Twisted by Joe Roach

Twisted

By

Joe Roach

Twisted

Web: Cadmuspublishing.com
Business email: admin@cadmuspublishing.com
ISBN# 978-1-63751-556-3

Book Catalog Info Categories:
  Crime/Thriller

Cadmus Publishing
CadmusPublishing.com

Chapter 1 Twisted

This book Twisted is about Joe's life and many experiences through out his life. Tamika he met at mango's she was a middle age lady a blonde very attractive her big breast and long blonde hair was what attracted him to her. With his blue eyes and what god pleased him with. Just remember size does matter. He starts by buying her a drink at the bar, then they get into a conversation about how women has never got the respect they deserve, Guys are liar's that only care about what they want. How he feels women are who deserves the most credit for all the great things in life .Women are the greatest thing life has to offer at least that's how he feels.

God made women to bless and be blessed, most men don't see it that way. They need to enjoy a woman make them happy, stop making women have to lie. guys know the truth and still they want the women to lie and say size don't matter. He tells Tamika how he had met a middle-aged woman when he was seventeen, how she took him in and how wonderful she was to him.

He explained how he was taught to be good to a woman and how to spoil a woman in special ways, how he enjoyed spending time with Dare and everything Dare taught him about what women like, Tamika knew he knew what he was talking about, when he said the first thing a guy needs to know is how to kiss a woman, a guy that knows how to kiss gets the pussy juice flowing, because the mouth is not the only place a woman likes to be kissed ,when he said this to her she smiled and said I'm listen you have my attention. First time ever she heard a guy say these things.

Joe was in his forty's attractive and had his charming ways with the lady's especially with his Jesus blue eyes.

The more he talk the more turned on Tamika was getting. She never met anyone like him before. She was itching to say to him come home with me. She ask him about coming back to her place? When they got to her place setting on the sofa she said she was uncomfortable but it had nothing to do with him, it was the thong she was waring she told him that it had her uncomfortable, for some reason it was rubbing her asshole raw. He tells her just to take it off if it was that uncomfortable.

Before she could say anything he had her skirt pushed up past her hips taking her panties off , seeing what a pretty pussy she had shaved with a blonde stubbled landing strip, he gets on his knee's In front of her she tells him no at first, he started at her thighs he kiss and suck her thighs with soft kisses and soft sucking with his lips as he work his way to her pussy. Now at this point she had changed her mind it felt so good she was OK with it.

He goes way beyond what others would to satisfy a women with his way of kissing that she could tell right away. He was taught very well, he did it way different than any one else. When Tamika felt his tongue inside her, she knew she'd been blessed the way he said women should be, this was the first time she felt blessed the way she was feeling him doing to her. She knew what she was doing with him was wrong because she didn't know him at all. But she'd never had guy to make her feel the way he had her feeling. She closed her eye's and said not a word, just let him do what he want because it was obvious he knew what he was doing and it was feeling good to her, he knew what he was doing nothing he had said was a lie. He was doing to her just what he'd been taught bye Dare when he was a teenager. What made her for get about everything was when he got his lips around her clit with his tongue circling it until her clit was rock hard, then he sucks her clit so soft stroking it with his mouth. That's when Tamika knew he was the one.

She had no problem with him doing what he was doing once her clit was in his mouth being stroked and suck softly, until she was ready to get off. Getting off was something she could not control at the this time. After a assume orgasm she said to him she was surely blessed and glad to had bump in to him. He said to her he was the one blessed for her to let him eat her beautiful pussy. It was getting late he had to be leaving out to head to Florida to pick up ten kilo's of cocaine. First he had to pick up the pretty little nineteen year old girl that was going to ride with him. Tamika didn't need to know all this, he told her he had business to take care of early the next day so he needed to go.

Tamika ask him what about you don't you want to get off? He said to her would love to but first he want to show her he's not there for his wants it's all about her is what he wants her to see. She ask before he left when could she see him again? He said he'd be back in town the first of the week he could stop bye then she said please do, she'd be waiting to see and hear from him.

They exchanged phone numbers then he left. The rest of the weekend she thought about nothing but him. Hoping he would call because she'd never met anyone like him before. She wanted to know everything about him. His round trip to Florida takes him thirty two hours. This trip took thirty six because he had to stop bye his place on the way back to fuck this young girl that was riding with him. While fucking Tabatha's pretty little young pussy She would beg him to take his big long dick out her little young pussy.

He'd been fucking Tabatha since she was seventeen years old she learn to beg from the first time he fucked her with, all the women say he has a donkey dick. At first it hurt like hell but felt so good and deep.

She was the young girl he enjoyed fucking and many other thing's he enjoyed doing with her. She was his ride or die girl she was his Bonnie and he was her Clyde. Trafficking Kilo's of cocaine from Florida to Virginia was what turned her on. Just the thought of being breaking the law got them off.

Chapter 2

Joe was born a outlaw that's the only life style he knew that and charming beautiful woman, also running from the law was what he enjoyed the most. Young lady's he liked fucking them that to him was for extra credit because he could. After dropping off the ten kilo's in Rocky mount doe run area. He called Tamika she picked up on the second ring. He let her know he was back in town if she wanted he'd drop bye? But first he needed to shower she said she'd be there just come on in when he got there the door would be open.

When he got there she was cutting her grass. It's miserable hot that day temperature in the ninety's maybe even a hundred degree's. She stop the mower got off to move some thing's that needed moving before she could finish mowing the spot she was mowing..

He set there in his black on black BMW convertible, He enjoyed watching her ass from behind when she would bend over in those spandex shorts, he'd watch her ass spread like a ass should spread when a beautiful ass bends over.

What he like even more than watching her bend over was that soaked with sweat T shirt she was waring, her big titties her nipples look like deer in head lights. nice pretty nipples firm big cantaloupe size titties. He like nothing more than imagining fucking her cantaloupe size titties. The things he could do with her titties floated through his mind like a cloud in heaven's sky's.

That white T shirt was stuck to her titties looking like she didn't have a shirt on at all. She would stand facing him, she'd wipe sweat from her head with her hand. Just as she seem to be teasing him with her big pretty titties.

She walked over to the porch took a seat in a rocking chair took two beers from the cooler, then motion for him to join her on the porch. As he walked up to the porch, she had a ice cold beer holding against her titties.

He took a beer from the cooler then had a seat in the rocking chair straight across from her. She removed that ice cold beer that she was holding against her titties, he watch the stem come from her shirt and her titties. Nipples looked hard enough to cut glass pretty and pink.

There he set in his Levi jeans no shirt covered in prison ink from neck down. She'd never seen him with out a shirt his tattoo's had her pussy throbbing she want to experience getting fucked bye the bad boy she was imagining he was with a big dick.

She said guy's are lucky they can walk around with out a shirt.

Joe said to her you can it's no one around but us? She said that wouldn't be to lady like to do that in front of him. Joe said to her it wouldn't be to lady like to him if she didn't since he'd already eat her pussy before. He said to her he was interested in seeing those titties with out a shirt.

Tamika said you want to see these as she pulled her T shirt over her head to take it off? Then she circles both of them with her hand around and beneath wiping away the sweat. His big blue Jesus eye's shine bright as the north star, looking at her big titties and pretty pink nipples. For a forty year old woman her titties look to be of a twenty year old girl that's how firm they look to be. They had to be at least a 40 DD perfect size for him to fuck , his dick was long enough he could fuck her in the mouth with the head of his dick at the same time. Yes he was blessed like that. She didn't know but she'd soon find out.

He told her she had the prettiest titties he had seen, she thank him then said do you want to suck my pretty pink nipples? Then she learned forwards towards him to kiss him on his lips. Just from that kiss her pussy was dripping wet. She stands up in front of him he leans forward to suck her nipples. She said they got to taste salty from the sweat? He said he would not have it any other way he lick her sweaty nipples before he suck them.

He reach both hands around got her bye both ass cheeks, he pull her closer as he took his tongue and lips he lick and suck her belly button while he looked up at her with is Jesus blue eye's.

She liked his blue eye's she'd never seen eye's as blue as his before. She said you got me dripping wet already. He said to her let me see how wet that pussy is? She said to him looks like I don't have any control over that? you going to do what you want, so go ahead. with his hands on her ass cheeks, with his hands he pulls down her shorts. She had no panties on.

Chapter 3

As Tamika goes to set down in her rocking chair he followed with his mouth, while he slides out of his rocking chair to his knee's on to the porch.

She puts both her legs over the arm of the rocking chair she lays back putting her pussy up so he can finish what he started. Joe was into young girls but this forty year old woman had a pussy with a taste he couldn't resist.

Exploring her slit with his tongue to find her clit, when he does he rubs his tongue over her clit to make it grow big and harder, so he can suck it with his lips into his mouth. At this point Tamika had relax while he suck soft and slow his tongue licking the tip of her clit. He knows bye the look on her face as he's watching her mouth and tongue movement, he feels her body tightened up she jerks, that jerk was the flood gate opening, he left the clit to go to the honey hole where he suck her sweet juices from her pussy she squirts into his mouth and on his face.

With ever squirting pump she jerk until she was drained, her leg's close tightly against his head, then slowly her thighs relax her head falls back on the rocking chair she jerks her final jerk. just as she had took her last breath.

He takes his dick out he pulls Tamika's ass closer to the edge of the rocking chair, she's relax with her head laid back her eye's is closed he puts the head of his dick inside her. Tamika opens her eye's she looks at his dick she said holly damn what a dick. He leans on in so his dick slides in until his balls is against her ass.

She said to God what did she do to deserve all this? He fucked her until he was ready to get off, she pleaded with him and god not to take it out, she ask him to stay deep inside her? He got off inside her as his dick went down her pretty pussy tightened up and pushed his dick out.

He finished cutting her grass while she cook burgers and hot dogs on the grill. There with her was where he stayed changing her life from being a good woman to being the kinda woman he's always wanted.

She was proud of his dick she measure his dick to see just how long it was, from his balls to the head he had a 11 1/2 inch dick.

Tamika had a daughter that did not care for Joe at all at first, Once she got to know him that would soon change.

Tamika like spoiling Joe she like giving him a bath while giving him a bath she like jacking him off with body wash or conditioner. Her daughter lived with her grandma. Come spring break she stayed with her mom. Her mom had the bathroom door locked while she was jacking him off in the tub like she like to do.

Her daughter was pissed off cause she was locked out!!!! So the next time Tamika left the bathroom door open. So her daughter wouldn't have a reason to get pissed off.

Tamika was jacking him off, her daughter comes in has a seat on the toilet, she lean forward to watch her mom jack Joe's dick. Joe liked her daughter to watch her mom jacking his dick that turned him on.

Her daughter was seventeen years old, she set there her pussy dripping wet watching her mom jack his long brown dick . When he was ready to cum Tamika held the head tight to build up pressure, when it cum it shot out under pressure onto her daughters arm the second shot was on her daughters leg.

After that was when everything between Tamika's daughter an Joe changed . The next day Tamika's daughter ask Joe if he'd like to go riding with her on her 4 wheeler back in the mountain? Tamika was happy to see her daughter wanted to spend time with Joe. Joe said sure he'd like to go riding with her on her 4 wheeler. She took him back in the mountain to a hunting cabin, they stop she help Joe into the window then he unlock the door for her to come inside. She like the way he had no problem breaking the law bye breaking into the hunting cabin, Tina being young she got turned on bye that, Joe unlock the door once he was inside to let Tina in. Tina walked in she took his hand turned him face to face with her, she kissed him she kiss just like her mom, her mom had to been to teach her to kiss. He ask her if her mom teach her to kiss? She ask why would he ask that? He said because you kiss great just like your mom. Tina said her mom teach her to kiss when she was fifteen.

They quickly undress she had a body that would call Jesus off the cross. Her ass was so perfect it held her pussy up off the bed just perfect for him to get to with his tongue lips and mouth, he did her the same way he did her mama the first time. Then he put his dick inside her pretty young shaved pussy pounding her pussy with her legs over his shoulders.

After many begs and pleas to God Tina beg Joe cums inside the same as he does her mama. Then his dick goes down and slides out. Being the outlaw bad boy he was he sucked Tina's cummy wet pussy. This drove her wild for him to do after whispering in her ear telling her what he was going to do while he was fucker her. That always seems to get a girl out of her circle when he does that young or older.

Tina said to him this was their secret because if her mom found out he fucked her she would be mad as fuck at the both of them, Joe agree this stayed between them. They got their self together then they went back to the house.

Chapter 4

Tamika was a therapist so she worked five day's a week. That worked out great for him now he was fucking Tina. Every morning after her mom left for work. Tina would come climb in her mom's bed naked with Joe.

Life for joe was great he had it made living there with Tamika, he didn't have to work he was fucking mom and baby girl how much sweeter could life get? Tamika had a two girl friends Terry and Tracie she introduce Joe to. Another big mistake Terry and Tracie were sister's they like to party.

Tracie and Terry ran into Joe at store he was getting gas in his black on black BMW convertible, Tracie was the wild one of the two, Tracie said to him while Tamika was at work be a good time for him to fuck her and her sister both?

Joe said to her he could do that just follow him to his place in Roach town, Tracie was down for it Terry said she didn't know then Terry said what the hell lead the way.

Joe like doing things like this it was like skip the game, wasn't no for play he knew what they wanted that was clear. This was going to be fun eating sisters pussy and fucking them both, he'd done a lot of thing's throughout his forty some year's of living. This was the first time he'd have sisters at the same time. Damn if he wasn't blessed he said to his self.

He could only imagine the thing's he would do to Tracie and Terry once they got to his place. When they got there Tracie was first to take off her clothes then started playing with her pussy while her sister and Joe watch while she lay in his king size bed.

Joe then got her bye her ankle's, he pulled her ass close to the edge of the bed leaving room for her feet to rest on the edge of the mattress with her knee's up open to both sides. Her sister Terry watch him go down between her sisters leg's. She watch as he licked her sisters pussy then her asshole he lick next.

Terry notice while he was licking and sucking her sister's asshole her sister's pussy juice got to flowing like honey. That turner Terry on she had never tasted her sisters pussy cum before, He looks at Terry he notices her rub her tongue over her top lip like she was hoping he'd let her take over an taste her sisters pussy cum. He moves from between her sisters legs she didn't hesitate a bit, she was on her knees between her sisters thighs sucking her sister's pussy, she like the taste of her sister's pussy cum. This is what the lady's do with Joe Roach smoking meth and snorting cocaine. while watching them kiss and make out he fuck them both when he was ready to cum they both shared his dick in their mouth back and forward until he cum, then with his cum in their mouth they kiss exchange his cum back and forward from one sisters mouth to the other before they swallow. This is the life Joe Roach lives, this is the reason for so many Hater's and the lawmen hate him.

Joe wants all the woman to know how much he respects them and home much they should mean to all men. He's truly one of a kind a great guy not a Hater like so many guy's are towards him. Because they can't be like him.

Most women have never squirt before with a guy, all pussy squirts you just got to know how to make it squirt, when a guy is only thinking about him like 99% of them do, not many woman experience squirting that's why.

That's a satisfaction ever woman needs to experience that's when she is more than satisfied. Squirt in his mouth what he can't swallow he'll spit out. He want stop until she is more than satisfied.

What he does with the women should be against the law, it's not if it was he'd be doing a life sentence, this life is all he knows getting high selling drugs spending time like this with the women young and older all women deserve more respect than most of them get from their man. Men treat women like slaves that's bullshit, women you should stand against them all of you got what they want, men are the weak one's, what most of them have to offer you for your great fullness is a little dick that ain't shit. Remember that the next time you feel like your man is disrespecting you, you all are being did respected bye a man with a little dick. You don't have to put up with that bullshit!!!!

Tamika daughter move back in with her mom after staying spring break with her mom and Joe. Tina had started making trips to Florida with Joe picking up kilo's of cocaine. She was liking his outlaw life style. She'd soon be eighteen.

Being free to do as she please now dressing the way Joe like for her to dress. Some say like a slut he says more like lady, while riding down the interstate her giving him head while he's driving. Her laying naked in the passenger seat with the top down getting a tan while riding down the interstate. This was the life style he liked. Him finger fucking her pretty pussy while he's driving, She like Cumming on his fingers then watch him lick her sweet cum from his fingers, this was the only kinda of life style he wanted to live.

Spoiling mama while she was home spoiling daughter while mama was at work. Plus he enjoyed Tamika friends Terry and Tracie while baby girl was in school and mama was at work. joes been Twisted his whole life. One blessing after another know wonder certain lawmen hate him.

Chapter 5

Terry stop bye one day while Tamika was at work and her
daughter was in school. What she was waring said everything that
needs to be said. she had a seat in the recliner she set back leaving
the recliner closed, she put her legs over the arms of the recliner,
Joe slides her ass close to the edge. He undresses down to his
boxer's then with out saying a word he's on his knee's his face
between her thigh's her ass is so thick it's got her pussy setting up
off the chair.

Both pussy & asshole already know what's about to happen,
betting on what one gets his tongue first, he starts with the asshole
her pussy starts flowing like a creek over flowing it's banks.

He inserts his nose in Terry's over flowing pussy. He could tell
she's never had anything like this done to her before. while he suck
her asshole, he breath through his nose making sweet wet pussy
noises escape from her pussy.

The harder he breath the loader the noises get as the noises
escapes. She's confused because her insides feel quivery he leaves
the asshole to take his nose from her pussy so he could suck up her
over flowing pussy juice that was gushing out like water fountain.

She'd cum unexpectedly she tries to get him to stop cause she
is shaky and nervous she's never felt anything like this before, he
has her bye her waist as he find's her clit, it's already rock hard he
sucks it the way girls like it, She wants to scream she doesn't she
afraid she going to pee if she does. That's how she feel's she tried
to set up to cup her hands over her pussy. He's looking up at her
he's sucking, he moves his head side to side telling her no don't

even try it let it go, she's holding back he can tell. She tries to relax she's never had a guy to show her pussy this much attention.

She never thought she'd be getting her pussy sucked like this bye her best friends boyfriend. She knows what she's doing is wrong but it feel's to good to stop.

He can tell bye looking up at her face expression with her mouth opening slowly her tongue rubbing across both of her pretty lips she's about to get off again.

She tells him here it comes she went to say it again, all she got out was here it, the flood gate open for the first time he had to abandon her pussy she squirted so hard he got choke, she kept squirting like a water fountain that was out of control then she pee uncontrollably.

He stands up he cough's he's choked, he gets unchoked, she's jerking then trembling all over. His dick is rock hard he slides down his boxer's, he pushes her leg's back he let's the head of his dick chose what hole that it wants, she look down and seen his dick, his dick doesn't look like it belongs to him, his waist and legs are ghost white, his dick and balls are brown, Strange how much it turned her on she liked it so much it was like being fuck bye a black dick, she's never done that before only fantasies about it.

She like watching Joe's brown dick disappear inside her white pussy, it gets her off again fast and hard . If you ask a white girl if she wants a black dick she will lie and say no. That's one of the biggest lies she will ever tell. Joe knows the truth because he was born with a brown dick.

That gets the white girls heart pumping just to watch it fuck them, he knows what most of the white girls like nowadays. Guy's it's a mind thing that makes a white woman get off to fantasies about, Joe gets to watch in real life how it gets them off. They can lie to you white guy's they can't lie to Joe what he see's and what he knows is a fact, the white girl's look at his dick the same way as a nigga dick. Terry screams she cums she squirts when he pulls his dick out after he cums deep inside her.

Terry laid her head back biting on her bottom lip, she looked him in his blue eyes she said five words. Please put it back in!!!

She looked him in his eye's just as she was in heaven's bedroom looking out, looking into his blue eye's, he put it back in inside her half hard, she Mon but didn't say a word she just noted her head, he knew he pushed her legs on back as he bottomed out inside her with his fat long half hard dick they both got off at the same time.

She no longer regrets what she's doing with her best friends boyfriend in her best friends recliner. This is sometimes how life play's out. Thing's like this happen a lot nowadays especially with Joe.

The king pin life style never seems to surprise him at what he finds his self getting into, when it comes down to sex with a beautiful woman.

God blessed him with so many ways to bless the lady's. Women have not been blessed like he continues to bless them one bye one, blessing as many that will let him bless them. Lady's if you never been blessed in these ways before? You with the wrong man.

Joe Roach will bless you just give a shout out to him. He's in prison right now for living this lifestyle. That's what the lawmen say but what it boils down to is having to much fun with the ladies.

Want be long he'll be back living this lifestyle again can't keep a good man down when he's blessed like Joe Roach has been his whole life. God blessed the right one cause he's not afraid or shy to share his blessing with all you lady's that's never been blessed like this.

Chapter 6

Joe might not know many things, one thing he does know is how much women should mean to the men in this world. They are priceless you can't put a price on the most beautiful thing god ever created. Women are the greatest thing God created with out women this world wouldn't be worth living in.

He doesn't say these things to win over the lady's, he says this because this is the truth about how important women really are to the world we are living in.

He feel's no man will go as far as he does, to show a woman how great they really are, and give them the respect they deserve and bless them they way they deserve to be blessed.

The reason for this book is for the lady's to know he thinks more for them than anything else, because he knows the hell they are put through just dealing with everyday life. Having to lie by saying size doesn't matter.

Women are put through hell. The men in this world make it a miserable world to live in for a lot of women, just because a man doesn't get his way he call's women bad names like sluts and whores.

That's the bullshit women have to deal with everyday.

The only time Joe finds peace is when he's between a woman's thighs and that big long brown dick in a sweet juicy pussy.

He'd met a young girl that he caught feelings for while he was out riding around on his black on black BMW convertible selling crystal meth and cocaine. not counting the other dozen he'd messed around with like Terry & Tracie and the three young girls he got pregnant while Tamika was at work..

He knew when she found out what he'd been doing he better have a plan to do something different. She told him when this relationship began better not be no fucked up bull shit. With in a year he's done all these things, including her daughter she's one of the young girl's that is pregnant. She is eighteen now thank god for that.

This would be the reason for Tamika to snap she might even put a bullet between his eyes. To do all these things he had done behind her back if she put a bullet right between his eye's. The law wouldn't blame her a bit.

Chapter 7

Knowing all that he had done while Tamika had been working some of it was going to come out. Two young girls pregnant one of them two was her daughter. It was three but Anna had a abortion that was the one he was so crazy over.

Anna was a beautiful girl she lived in Altavista she was seventeen when they met she was quickly pregnant. Her mom & Dad made her get a abortion.

They forbid Anna to continue to see him. Anna's birthday was coming up, he had plan to pick Anna up at the end of her driveway, they were going to Daytona Florida for bike week on her eighteenth birthday.

Anna had been sneaking off saying she was with a friend the whole time she was with him making his run to Florida and back. That was when she ended up pregnant.

His plans were pick up Anna then head for Daytona Florida spend a week there partying with Anna showing her a great time for her birthday. Then head to Miami to pick up ten kilo's of cocaine to take back to Virginia.

He picked up Anna, her beauty and everything else about her he was crazy about. Around her parents she dressed so proper because of how she was raised and who she was a preacher's daughter. When she was with Joe she could be her self the way she acted the way she dressed was totally the opposite than she was raised.

Twisted by Joe Roach

That hot July day he picked Anna up at the end of her driveway, while her mom & dad was at work, she was dressed the way she knew he liked her to dress. Most would say slutty that's what Joe was into, beautiful girl's being there self. A good girl turn bad this was the life style she like experiencing with him. The thing's she would experience with him very ungodly things.

When he picked her up she was waring a two peace bikini with a bows tied above her hips on both sides. And her bikini top had one bow tied in the front between her c cup beautiful titties. She was tan all over even her titties her ass & pussy.

Her beauty was of a Angel her beautiful body her long brown hair and those big brown bedroom eyes. That said only one thing to him come fuck me with that big long fat brown dick. She was so into him because she could talk to him about any and everything, he never judged her for the thing's she did like other guy's would when they didn't get their way. They spread rumor's all around that she was a slut. poor little girl was a preacher's daughter give her some respect.

The reason the guys called her a slut was because she got drunk on wine one night, at a home coming football game party her and her girlfriend snook out her parents to go to.

She was waisted on cheap wine mainly Boones Farm. She let the whole football team take turns fucking her, that's the first time she'd got pregnant and got a abortion. She told Joe this he didn't judge her he liked her even more. poor little preacher's daughter show her some respect preacher's daughters like dick too.

Joe didn't judge her for this kind of behavior he just showed her the love he had and felt for her, he knows how cruel and hurtful guys can be towards women, especially when they not getting any play or pussy when they want it.

Guys don't like when they not in control, they could not understand how he was always with a beautiful girl? They should try not calling them sluts and whores maybe they can be with a beautiful girl.

Surely he knew what he was doing when it come to pulling the lady's, he was a down to earth guy that never cared what women did. He couldn't control his own life. What reason would he want to control anyone else's? Just live enjoy life experience different thing's. That's his way of living life.

Guys say he encouraged bad behavior for the lady's when he's only helping them experience different things in life they never get to experience with any other guy. Guys are Hater's!

While riding down interstate 85 south with Anna . She had the seat laid back he puts his right hand on her thigh to feel the beauty he seen laying there.

...

There Anna lay with both bows untied and her bikini between her legs laying in the seat, her pretty tan shave pussy looking so peaceful in the passenger seat, her bikini top she'd took off and tossed into the back of his black on black BMW convertible with the top down. She had on her high dollar shades she lay there looking like a angel with her eyes closed, while her body tan going down interstate 85 South towards Daytona beach Florida just outside of Virginia headed to enjoy bike week for her birthday.

It was a beautiful cite just to see how beautiful Anna truly was just being her. Something she could never be able to be with most of the guys. With out being called a slut when they got mad because they didn't get their way. If you couldn't have your way with Anna you had to be a clown. She was the easiest girl Joe had met to get along with. What Joe really enjoyed about Anna was the way she took all his big dick to be such a young girl , he like fucking her with her legs over his shoulder's while he was hammering her with every inch of his 11 1/2 inch dick his balls smack hard against her ass making a clapping sound every time they landed hard against her ass. He slowed it down to grind his body to her to make sure her clit got the attention that it needed and deserved to get off the way she like to get off with all his dick inside her.

Chapter 8

This was the story of his life and what the girls liked about him was his lifestyle. No other guy's girls could talk to like they could him.

Near Georgia Anna wakes up they stuck in a traffic jam, she sets up to look at what was going on. Vehicles beside them four lanes of traffic, started honking their horns at the beauty they seen, her without a top Joe could only imagine the horns that would be blowing if she was standing up and they could see her beautiful body.

She just smiled and waved at the motorists before reaching in the back to get her bikini top to put it on. Once she got her top on she tied her bikini bottom on both sides above her beautiful hips.

Once traffic started moving she said to Joe she had to pee, so he got off on the next exit, he was hoping she would hold it at least until he could get through the state of Georgia.

He had a ounce of cocaine in the trunk inside a dummy car battery, he didn't think they'd find it if he was pulled over, he didn't want to take a chance, but he was going to have to for Anna to pee she said she had to pee bad.

Georgia is the worst state for pulling over vehicles with Virginia plates. It's like they know people from Virginia are up to no good.

This contraption he had in the trunk he'd come up it was a super size battery mounted in his trunk hooked up to look functional but a dummy. Many times he'd had the dog's sniff his car it was funny to watch the dog hit just as they were train to do. Sniff hit set down the dog would keep doing this, the lawmen said to him Joe Roach give it up we know it's here, we going to find it when we do you going down unless you tell us now where you got it hiding?

They would search his black on black BMW convertible inside and out hood and trunk never cross their mind the battery they were seeing was a dummy the whole time.

You know they know what he's talking about what a damn fool he made of the lawmen back home, damnest fools he'd ever seen calling their self lawmen yea right nigga please.

Joe pulls in at the gas station up off exit 56 on interstate 85, he pulls up to the gas pumps to fuel up while Anna goes in to pee. He reach her a $100 told her to get him a soda and what ever she wanted plus a tank of gas.

As she walked across the parking lot he watch her ass she was reaching back pulling her bikini out of her ass crack. every step she took her ass was chewing on her bikini. She had a ass so beautiful only god could have been responsible for her ass to be so fine.

As she walk bye two lady's they to stop turn to look at her ass cause it was that fine, she paid then return he pump gas then back on the interstate headed to Daytona Florida.

She took out her king James Bible while he drove she read from the bible his favorite Job.

Anna reads to him about job and how Jobs kids were killed, his animals getting took his servants getting killed what a bitch his wife was telling him to curse God. After all this job was still loyal to God. Job is Joe's favorite in the bible.

Joe had issues he never talked about he enjoyed the drug lifestyle pretty women lots of sex and corrupted behavior. That's what he lived for. Leaving all his problems in his mind to help him destroy his self.

Other than these issues he had going on, he was pretty slick when it come to transporting drugs he always had his vehicles in his sisters name, that way when and if he got pulled over he'd use his older brother's name, his brother was one of the good ones that never been in any trouble. His sister was the same way, so if he got pulled over when the law ran the plates it come back to her. When they ran his brother's info that he knew bye heart that came back as clean as a whistle. They had no right to think about searching the vehicle.

He knew how the law worked as long as they didn't know he was Joe Roach. If so he was fuck from the start, that's why he knew his brother's info bye heart. Fuck the law drive with kilo after kilo running the interstate.

He got pulled over one time coming back on his black on black BMW convertible he was speeding, not paying any attention to the speed, he was rubbing Anna's thigh before he started circling her clit with his index & third finger. watching her out the side of his eye enjoy what he was doing, she cores her beautiful titties in both her hands as he cores her clit.

paying her all the attention got him pulled over, she lay there naked top and bottom untied pretended to be asleep. When the lawman sees her beautiful body it's no way he'd write a ticket.

He pulls over to the shoulder of the interstate he drops his wallet between the drivers seat and the console. So he can act as if he'd misplace or lost his wallet, giving him a reason to give them his info but really he was giving his brother's info.

Looking in the rearview mirror he could see the state "woman" walking up on the passenger side, He didn't expected the state police to be a lady. He says not a word Anna's laying there as the State police woman is walking to the passenger side.

She's a hot red head state police woman. She see's Anna laying there like a angel asleep, she takes a good look then ask for his drivers permit? He reaches for his wallet in his back pocket then he acts surprise its not there.

He shakes Anna to wake up to ask if she seen his wallet, Anna acts surprise they were pulled over she said to the lady officer sorry. The lady said that's OK. Just cover up if you don't mind.

Anna tied her bikini bottom then her bikini top then set up in the seat, Joe said ma'am can I just give you my info I can't find my wallet must have misplaced it.

The pretty lady officer took his info.

Chapter 9

She said hang tight she'd be right back, she walk back to her car Joe is nervous because it's ten kilo's of cocaine in the back seat drivers side in a duffel bag.

Anna is nervous she said if we get caught you taking the blame!!! Joe said OK fine just shut up please!!! Anna laid the seat back just as she was resting, this beautiful lady officer walks up on Anna's side again to avoid traffic, she let's joe off on a warning for speeding.

She said to Anna hey sweety just wanted to say nice I like that, Anna said thank you, the lady officer said no problem, be careful pulling out. Then she said she would block traffic so they could pull out on to the interstate. Them were the good old day's now he's old and grey the memories come back to remind him what he's missing. This same behavior sent him to prison to serve his second ten year sentence.

When they got to Daytona he got them a hotel room for the week right on the strip $1,000 for the week that was cheap for bike week. you got to think this was back in the early ninety's.

It was motorcycles parked up and down the strip, every restaurant was packed every bar was packed, beautiful women every where many of them topless.

The strip is right on the beach it's bar after bar up and down the strip. After getting her bags and Joe got his things he open the trunk unlatch the battery he open the top of the battery he reach in got the ounce of grade A cocaine. With that he was hoping to meet someone else that wanted to party with them, like another pretty girl depended on Anna just have to wait and see.

He had mentioned to Anna about him and her and another girl? Anna didn't say no but at the same time she didn't say yes either.

They quickly put their things away Joe cut him and her out a line, the line he cut out was big enough to get a elephant high as fuck, Anna said damn Joe you sure? this looks like a lot to snort at one time!!!!!

Joe said trust him she was going to need a line that big to fit in at the club during bike week. She said OK so she snorted half the line up one side her nose then the other half up the other side.

He snorted his the same way they then showered together had mad sex in the shower, she was a pro at taking every inch of his 11 1/2 inch dick. Where it all went he didn't know one thing he did know it surely felt good inside her. He like bending her over in the shower forcing her head in the corner against the wall, keeping her head push down while he pounded her back out. Young girls listen to him when he said stay bent over that's what she did for as long as it took for him to get off inside her.

Her ass was so fine bent over her pretty hips with his hand grip above her hips both sides around her waist, her pussy was taking a well deserved beating. Anna was different than all the other girls he been fucking, she had no gag reflex he could tell her to get on her knee's put the back of her head against the wall. He could throat fuck her half hard when it got rock hard she'd lay on the bed on her back with her head hanging over the side, head hold her bye both sides of her head as he smack his balls off her chin that's the way she like getting throat fucked bye his long brown dick.

After getting off in her in the shower he got out while she doused her pussy for it to fresh and clean before they hit the strip, she had just turned eighteen she was ready to celebrate. Her body alone was her ID that she was old enough to drink.

She had a body to be proud of and she was proud of it. She like showing it off. Joe like watching her show it off. That would be topless for Anna, that would get her lots of attention and permission to drink mix drink's.

If you never been to bike week in Daytona you need to go because never again you get to enjoy a week of the kind of fun you find at bike week in Daytona.

This whole week is topless for the lady's it's a lot of fun. If you never watch two girl make out you've not been to bike week in Daytona.

Bike week was where he watch Anna make out with a girl, Anna said it was her first time Joe found that hard to believe after watch her make out with a girl at the bar rubbing titties sucking face. She been with a girl before many times the way it looked.

Anna confessed she had been making out with girl's since she was fifteen.

Anna said only three girls she'd made out with. The way Anna and this girl were enjoying each other that cocaine might come in handy to take it to the next level when they get back to the hotel room.

Chapter 10

That first night in Daytona So far look very promisingly exciting. Anna's beauty attracted more beautiful girls. Like the one she made out with at the club. The girl Anna was making out with was in her mid twenty's. She want more than just kissing and caressing Anna's titties, she whisper in Anna's ear to tell her boyfriend to follow them into the lady's room.

So he did when they got into the lady's room She had him to set Anna on the sink where this beautiful blonde would show her thing's between her legs that Joe enjoyed watching.

One thing about a woman they know what other girls like. They know how to make a girl feel better than most men. When Tamara was done Anna was shaking uncontrollable. She was as weak as a kitten this he like to see, he's never watch two girls before he like this very much.

That week in Daytona was a week they would never for get. Anna got to experience many thing's from having sex with a girl , to getting double dick bye Joe and a guy she picked out to double dick her with Joe.

Growing up Anna was always told not to be having sex with black guy's, which she'd already experience that with the black guy's on the high school football team. She was waisted when she did that so it was very little she remembered about that night.

That's what she wanted to do again Joe was fine with it he'd done it with another older lady before, the only thing different was the older lady suck one while the other was hitting her from the back, then they would switch out to cum in the older lady's mouth.

Anna had a pretty pussy that would take two dicks that's what she wanted, she had been double dick bye Joe and his cousin before, she wanted Joe's dick and a black dick in her pussy at the say time.

They both had a large dick that's what Anna was hoping for Joe laid down on the bed Anna got on top she put his big dick inside her sweet wet pussy. Then came the black dick took a few attempts before it went in, it was a tight fit it felt great to her and Joe, he didn't have no control over his dick Cumming with a dick pumping her pussy against his dick he had no say so over that the big dick jacked him off quick inside her then pushed Joe's out as his dick went down.

Unlike him and his cousin they came in her at the same time. With the pussy being filled full of two monster size dicks wasn't but minutes before Joe cum. once his dick was push out the way the black dick pounded away at her white pussy.

This was the experience she was hoping for her Joe and the black guy had sex multiple times that night. She liked when the black guy got on top of her folded her leg's back so she could see his dick pounding away at her white pussy.

Lot's of white girls like this but they have to lie to keep the white guy's from crying. That's one reason all the girl's like Joe so much he had no reason to cry he had a big dick also.

Anna got to do a lot off thing's with him she would never get to do with other white guy's. That goes for pretty much all the girl's he's been with.

Being like this and not caring to share was some of the thing's him and another older woman did together. Color was never a factor in his life. The same with Anna that was one of the reasons he was so foolish over her. The thing's she would do with him.

After that week in Daytona with Anna it was time to head to Miami to pick up ten kilo's of cocaine and head back to Virginia.

Anna's beauty kept his mind in a whirl wind thinking of all the thing's she was willing to do with him, seeing her beautiful body as they drove the interstate, guy's in big rig's trying to keep up to look at her in the passenger seat of his black on black BMW convertible. That turned him on to do all this with a beautiful girl like Anna.

Anna would suck him off going down the interstate while trucker's kept beside them to watch.

When Joe got back to Virginia Tamika ran into him at the store, she was more pissed of that he had ran off than she was at all the things she had heard, she had found out her daughter was pregnant but she was told it was bye someone else. That surprised him her daughter kept it real to protect him.

She wanted him to come back she said she would enjoy being his therapist. She'd like to hear all about his life that's been kept from her. She also said she felt they could experience life to a whole different level if that's what he wanted. Hearing her say that got the wheel's rolling inside his head. Anna was back staying at her mom & Dad at the time they had work thing's out for her to stay an finish school. She could but he had to pick up at the end of the driveway. They said he reminded him of gangster drug dealer. Lots of people said that about Joe. Why would they say that?

While Anna was back in good grace with her family he'd move back in with Tamika. The way she's talking sounds promising and very interesting. Does she even know what door she's about to open?

She'd not had a patient like Joe Roach she wanted him to tell her everything, she has no clue what she is about to hear, he likes talking about his life to a woman he's in a relationship with, he uses this as a opportunity to kick their sex life in high gear.

When he tells her about all that young pussy she's going to feel like she's got to do more because she's going to feel like it's a competition. Older woman don't like to think these young girls can take their man. Joe knows this so buckle up he's ready to start manipulating his way to get her to do things he would never expect her to agree to, it's a game for him now.

Chapter 11

She's never met anyone like Joe before, she can't figure him out he has her brain washed bye the thing's he tells her. She's waring shorter skirt's and tops now that show more of her big 40 DD breast. She play's over and over in her mind while playing with her self she visions certain things he's told her that turns her on.

Her favorite so far has been about Anna how him and the black guy double dick Anna while they were in Daytona. That she visualized the most about. Nothing like this she has ever been told before from a patient over the twenty years of being a therapist. She likes it she wants to try all these thing's, does this mean she's going throughout a midlife crisis? Joe surely hopes so that would be great and perfect timing. To corrupt a therapist that would be right up his alley.

Since he's been back everything about him is different the way he eats her pussy the way he whispers all these ungodly thing's in her ear while he's making love to her turns her on more than she's ever been turned on her whole life.

While he's grinding his body against hers with his long fat dick inside her whispering in her ear she's visualizing in her mind what he's whispering in her ear at that moment. Sends her into a uncontrollable orgasm.

It's like he's inside her head making her want to do all these thing's he whispers in her ear. She likes it she wants it she's going to do everything he has her visualizing in her mind.

She thinks about all this driving down the road she plays with her pussy, he's got her twisted in her head, is it him or is it a part of life she's been missing?

Most the women that Joe knows that is this sexual active in their mind is doing the drug he keeps a unlimited supply of crystal meth.

To hear of this behavior from a therapist that doesn't do drugs means one thing Joe has her twisted with all these ungodly thing's he whispers in her ear.

She can't wait to get off work to get back home to hear more about him and the things he has done. He had told her so many ungodly things she was finger fucking her pretty pussy at work at her desk.

She started going to church every Sunday faithfully to pray and ask god to for give her for all the ungodly things she had going through her mind that her and Joe talked about that was turning her on all day while she was trying to work.

A month into this knew unusual relationship he was out dropping off crystal meth at the hotel when he ran into a young white girl he knew. she went bye booty short's she was with her black girlfriend name Diamond.

These two girls both young and beautiful they didn't do drug's they like to drink mix drink's and party. The thing's they like to do with each other Joe decided to get a room an party with booty shorts and Diamond that Friday night.

The three of them show up at the club together called corn beef this turns out to be a night he never wants to for get. These young girls rock that club then latter they rock that hotel room.

He's turned his phone off because Tamika is blowing it up trying to find out where he's at. She knows he's up to something when he has his phone turned off. She is so pissed off at the same time she's so turned on bye what she has going through her mind he's probably doing. She plays with her pussy dripping wet until she gets her self off.

Then she's back blowing up his phone leaving messages one after another he turn his phone back on the next morning. Before he goes any further he wants to say, all these stories about his past is all true to the best of his knowledge unless he's forgotten something to tell you about. If anyone thinks they are more twisted than him all he can say is they might need therapy also.

Early the next morning he turns his phone on to find he has 101 text messages from Tamika. They started out with how much she hated him then as they went on through the night she told him how much she was in love with him and she wanted to be apart of what ever he was doing.

His phone rings it's ten o'clock Saturday morning it's Tamika he answers, she has changed her attitude. She wants him to come home or tell her where he's at so she can come to him?

He said you'd have to be here to understand what this young black pussy has turned me onto. Her and her friend booty shorts you need to meet. He ask booty shorts and Diamond if they mind if he face time his therapist slash girlfriend? They both say go ahead they would like to meet her. Tamika said to him please do. So that's what he did he face time Tamika so she could watch everything live that was going on. Tamika was not expecting these young girls to be so young and beautiful.

This is the only way Joe Roach does it she would soon understand why he is the way he is. Live on face time.

These two young girls both around the same age with bodies of a angel. We're standing bye the bed both naked rubbing on each others titties and ass.

This was the first time ever his therapist had ever seen a pretty white girl make out with a pretty black girl, just seeing them young and beautiful naked had her pussy throbbing as her pussy juice over flow her pussy and asshole, as she watch them making out standing bye the king size bed in the hotel room.

Joe set the phone directly across from the bed on the TV stand as Diamond and booty shorts climbed onto the bed. Diamond laid on her back while booty shorts the white girl climb like a pussy cat between her legs. Booty shorts with her beautiful body her ass is up doggy style her back arch like broke back mountain so his therapist could see her pretty pussy and her asshole looking back at his therapist on the screen.

Booty shorts starts bye softly kissing Diamonds pretty black thighs slowly making her way to Diamonds pretty black pussy that's already dripping wet.

Chapter 12

When they were done booty shorts and Diamond said to his therapist you should join us sometime? His therapist wanted to but at the same time she was feeling a little jealousy of Joe being with them young girls.

Joe stops the face time he takes the phone into the bathroom to talk in private with his therapist. He can tell right away she starting to get into her feelings about these young beautiful girls. She tells him she can't keep doing this it was destroying her mental status. She liked it to much to continue so just call off their relationship not to call or come back around.

With out any argument with her he said OK good bye then hung up the phone. For him to just hang up like that pissed her off, she quickly called him back, he said hello she said you a peace of shit just wanted you to know that, he said OK then he hung up the phone again on her.

She gets her self together she flips the mattress on the bed because she had soaked it with pussy cum watch Joe fuck Diamonds pretty black pussy. After flipping the mattress and changing the bed sheets she calls him back more pissed than before.

Diamond answers his phone Tamika ask to speak to Joe, Diamond said he'll have to call you back unless you want me to face time you so you can watch him fucking booty shorts in her pretty ass.

That add fuel to fire that was inside her, she held it together she said please just have him to call me back.

Joe still hasn't called her back yet it's been over two hours now. She calls him back now his phone is turned off. More pissed off than ever she rides to Day's inn to find Joe.

When she gets there she spots his car setting around back backside parked in front of room 128. She Parks beside his black on black BMW convertible. She gets out she walks up to the door of room 128.

She nocks on the door Diamond opens the door she recognizes this lady from face time it Joe's therapist slash girlfriend. Tamika ask for Joe?

Diamond said he's busy at the moment double dicking booty shorts with my brother Q. You welcome to come in and watch if you like? His therapist comes in she sees booty shorts straddle a black guy riding him Joe behind her pumping his dick both dicks in booty shorts pussy at the same time.

She was mad on the way there but now she was liking what she was seeing them doing to booty shorts. Booty shorts was begging and pleading for them both to cum inside her at the same time.

Diamond rubs his therapist on her ass she said to his therapist have you ever had a black girl to eat your pussy? His therapist said no. Diamond said relax while I help relieve all your stress she started helping his therapist to get undressed.

Then Diamond told her to lay down beside Booty shorts on the king size bed, she did like she was told Diamond then started eating her white pussy. While his therapist watch Joe and Q double dick booty shorts that alone made her want to cum, when they both cum inside booty shorts pretty white shave double dick pussy, His therapist uncontrollably scream as she cum and squirt all over Diamonds beautiful black face.

Once they had pump booty shorts pussy with both of their cum at the same time booty short rolls over she lays on her back on the bed Joe and Q gets up from the bed, Diamond's face covered with his therapist pussy cum she goes to the bathroom to get a wet rag to wash off her face.

His therapist did something she never done before while Booty shorts lay there smoking a cigarette his therapist roll's over between Booty shorts leg's she's never eat pussy before she wanted to taste the cum in booty shorts pussy.

This was the life Joe lived for. His therapist first experience eating a cum filled pussy had her very much twisted from that day forward.

Watching her eat booty shorts cummy pussy turned Joe and Q on both with a hard dick they climb back on to the bed with Tamika when she was finished eating Booty shorts pussy.

Took several attempts before they got both dicks inside Joe's therapist slash girlfriend Tamika, when they did she liked it and wanted both them to get off inside her just as they did with booty shorts.

She was no longer agree at Joe she was more satisfied than she'd ever imagine she could be. the way two dicks felt inside her pussy at the same time was a feeling she could never explain.

Before she left the hotel room she told Joe he better have his ass home soon like in one hour, she said she was sorry for being so angry earlier when she said what she said about it being over.

Chapter 13

He got his self together then went home it was Saturday night Tamika totally satisfied and glad he's home. She wants to hear more about his wild outlaw life.

So he tells her about this one time back when he was selling crystal meth he went to deliver a eightball to a guy he'd been selling to for a while.

This guy had a beautiful blonde girlfriend he had been wanting to fuck for sometime. The guy had got in a accident his leg's was broke he was in a wheelchair.

Joe said he delivered the eightball of meth he set around with the guy and his pretty girlfriend getting high, The guy's girlfriend kept making eye contact with him behind her boyfriend's back, one time she was standing behind her boyfriend she raised her shirt up showed Joe her beautiful titties smiled then put her shirt back down.

Damn what pretty titties she had he could tell she was a natural blonde, because of her nipples pretty and pink. He said his friend that was in the wheelchair wheeled his self into the bathroom to take a piss.

The guy's girlfriend laying on the bed she quickly pulled her shorts down so he could see what a pretty shaved pussy she had. So he quickly took a butcher knife from the kitchen, he jam the knife between the bathroom door and the door jam to lock him in the bathroom.

While he was raising hell telling them to stop joking around Joe was putting dick to his girlfriend, the pussy was so good Joe left her boyfriend stuck in the bathroom, he took the guy's girlfriend with him when he was done fucking her.

The next day he was arrested for abduction for locking the guy in the bathroom against his will. The police didn't care for Joe to begin with they just wanted him put away.

He was held a week with out bond, the girl went back to her boyfriend, Joe hated that cause her pussy was so good he would have married that girl.

Tamika ask was the pussy that good? He said well not really but at the time he thought so.

Tamika ask how much time did he end up pulling for that? He said two year's . Tamika ask what did he do while he was in jail for the two years?

He told Tamika that was a story she would have to wait to hear cause he wanted to eat her pussy then make love to her. She was always good with that. quickly they started making out then he went down on Tamika wet cummy pussy from where she'd been double dick earlier bye Q & Joe.

Everything about him turned her on he made her want to crawl of Herr skin with his twisted ways of satisfying her pussy completely.

After sex he laid beside her in bed he said he want to take her to the sex store the next day to buy some toy's for her to experience and enjoy.

She's never been inside a sex store before she ask Joe what kind of toy's he was thinking about? He said to trust him it's going to be a lot of toys she's going to like.

The reason the guys didn't care for him was the snake in the grass he was. Everyone knew he was blessed in size cause people talk. women especially always talking about what big pretty dick he has. That alone made him well known in the county he was born and raised. Amongst a lot of Hater's.

Certain lawmen has serious personal issues with him, one especially he thinks Joe done donkey dick his mama. This little dick lawman can't see straight he's so damn pissed off with Joe Roach.

This certain lawman tries to get Joe a life sentence just for J walking on the sidewalk. Even if Joe hasn't donkey dicked his mama's back out with his damn near foot long dick, her son the little dick lawman thinks he did and he's out for revenge.

There's another lawman Joe knows that doesn't live far from where Joe was born and raised, Joe went to school with his wife he hates Joe Roach cause he knows Joe was always looking at his wife pretty ass when her and Joe was in school.

If Joe could have fuck that pretty hot ass blonde she surely wouldn't be married to that clown of a lawman she's married to.

Joe seen her at the store a few days ago walking across the parking lot, She's around fifty years old and still she had that ass. He thought to his self she need's this big fucking dick in her life.

He could tell that little dick lawman was doing nothing for that fine ass, just bye the way she twisted as she walk past, even her ass was saying to Joe please fuck me Joe. At least that's what he thought it said. Just wanted his neighboring lawman to know how he looked at his wife's ass still after all those years.

Chapter 14

He's helped a lot women experience life, It's nothing wrong with experiencing different things in life, A lot of women are deprived of so much in life they miss out on, trying to be a good honest woman while their man miss treats them mentally and physically. Mental abuse is just as bad as physical abuse. It's still abuse.

While they home raising kid's like they feel like its their job to do as most women do, Their man is making a fool of them bye fucking their friends and any thing else he can get his dick in.

Men are about as sorry as a person can get, then they have the nerve to call women sluts and whores. If a woman is a slut or a whore it most likely comes from having to do with a peace of shit man.

Sunday morning around ten o'clock. She's gets up and gets dressed the way José likes. She's waring a short summer skirt outfit like she would not be caught dead in before she met him. It was a cheap dollar store cotton summer outfit, with no panties the thin cotton skirt barely covered her ass cheeks. No bra with a lot of her size 40 DD titties showing just the way he liked. Some say slutty Joe says beauty if you got it girl flaunt it don't hide it be proud of it.

She enter the bedroom he didn't say a word after seeing how she was dressed, the way she was dressed spoke for it self. He took her bye the hand leads her to the bed he set's her down he puts his index finger to his lips indicate not to say a word.

He pushed her back slowly onto the bed he wanted to suck her just seeing her dressed the way she was, she'd never dressed for anyone to see the way she dressed for him. Ten minutes latter she was squirting cum and peeing all over his face that's how turned on she had him to suck her pussy that good to make her get off this hard in such a short notice. It's done got to the point nothing any more surprised her that he would do, cause he'd do anything at any given time. That made her get off like no other man has ever got her off, he didn't think about him his dick he had train his dick to get it self off just knowing what he was doing for them. He's train his dick to act accordingly and that's how it act's as it pumps it self back soft on its own just as it was inside her. Women deserve for men to be this way that tells them how turned on she turns them on being the woman they love.

He's easy to satisfy he's satisfied just bye satisfying her, his dick will cum he don't have to put it in her it will cum while he's eating pussy woman say he's got a magical dick. He's got enough dick to tittie fuck her and eat her pussy at the same time. What man you know can come close to doing that?

After eating her pussy his face covered with pussy juice and cum he straddles her belly then tittie fucks her while she sucks the head of his dick. Big dick to tittie fuck her 40 DD and get the head suck at the same time.

When he gets off, Tamika who never like sucking dick before he came along, now she doesn't waist a drop. Women change for a man that does special thing for them.

This is how he started her Sunday morning in the bed room. Now the dick and pussy was totally satisfied he drove her in his black on black BMW convertible to the dick store orange avenue Roanoke Va.

She was shy at first when they walked in she seen hundreds of different size dicks white guy dicks and black guy dicks hanging on the wall. All that shyness quickly went away, she spotted a white dick lap with a big dick and big balls that felt as real as it gets. This guy dick lap had a asshole also that felt like a real one just begging to be fucked in the ass.

She said this is the one that she wanted she want to ride that big dick feel how real it feel's inside her. She paid $300 for that dick lap then she got some platinum dick oil. A battery powdered dick ring, battery power annual bead's. She could not wait to get back to her bedroom to ride her dick lap, he could tell this dick store could become a addiction for her. Once again he felt blessed to have her for his woman.

When they got back home she quickly went into the bedroom, she quickly tore open the box her dick lap was in. She tossed the box on the floor the dick lap she laid on to the bed, she open the dick oil she oil the dick good, she pulled her short summer out for over her head and tossed it on to the floor, she climb on the bed straddles her dick lap backwards so she could watch it as she started the big dick inside her while Joe watch it disappeared into her pretty pussy plum to the balls. she rub the big set of balls with oil as he watch her ride that dick, she squirted dick oil up the asshole then motion for Joe to fuck it with his big dick in the ass.

He had no problem with that he gets on the bed she leans back as she oils up his dick she helps his dick find the wet oil soaked asshole. Then she watch as she watch the head of his dick disappeared inside the ass of the dick lap, Joe said this feels good, she rode the dick while she watch Joe fuck the asshole of her dick lap.

When he was ready to cum in the asshole he buried it deep she cum on the dick watch him come in her dick laps asshole. This is the truth if you lady's think he's lying just go to the dick store buy a dick lap and he will show you how he fucks it in the ass.

This is some of the reason women like Joe as much as they do he explores every opposition when it has to do with sex. That was how the dick store adventure went that Sunday for him and Tamika.

This is why you never see Joe Roach without a smile on his face. He's always a happy person living the life he lives why wouldn't he be?

No one lives as good as Joe Roach, that's a fact.

Back to telling Tamika about the two years he had to serve for the abduction charge.

Serving his first two-year sentence for abduction.

Chapter 15

Joe's upset cause he got two years behind that bull shit. But still thirty years latter he thinks about how good that pussy was while he is writing this book. It wasn't the justice system back then in the county he was born and raised, the Justice court system in the county he was born and raised was always fare. It was certain lawmen that had issues with him the way he lived and the things he did, like donkey dicking his fare share of pretty women. Still he had it made the judge recommended him stay in the county to do his time at a old prison camp. Camp 24 that was run bye the sheriff back then, Joe was born and raised knowing everyone that work there. He lived just fifteen minutes from there, doing time at that camp was like a vacation, The sheriff had him helping clean up storm damage on the park way. This was back when it was a good honest sheriff running thing's. Nothing like nowadays a corrupted sheriff with nothing but corrupted lawmen.

He was the only one the sheriff trusted to run a chain saw, because the sheriff knew that's what Joe was raised doing with his family being some of the biggest loggers in Virginia.

Every day he worked he earn a extra day, depending what sergeant was working he could get three days for one. That's how good they were to him there. Joe had a beautiful red head girl he was seeing while he was out on bond. Bonnie was her name she was a beautiful young lady in her late twenty's, she had to daughters they were little girls, they really like Joe, he was good to them he got the oldest one her first bike and teach her to ride it.

He got the youngest one her first tricycle at the same time he didn't buy one something and not the other one, he was good to those girls, Bonnie their mom was a wonderful and great woman,

She was one that he let get away. She come to visit him on visit day that was Sunday she bring the girl's to visit.

She come during the week and meet him on the parkway where he was cleaning up storm damage. The correctional officer he grew up around would let him meet up with her at the visiting center on the parkway at lunch time on the low. They had forty five minutes to hike in the woods hang out you know what grown ups do.

She was good to Joe even though he was a hound dog that would never be tamed. She tried but even in prison he'd find away to fuck the preaches daughter.

That's what ended their relationship Joe fucking the preaches daughter. He can only blame his self for messing up what he had with Bonnie.

Tamika ask him was you in prison or in day care? He said that was prison life for him back then, he and his family were well known in the county he lived in everyone liked him but certain little dick bastard lawmen.

As long as he was charged and tried in the county he was born and raised, the court system was always fare he couldn't complain. He never complained even when he got time back then the judge recommended him to do it at the old prison camp.

There was this fine as red head that was a c.o back then, she was a couple year's older than Joe was. She grew up coming to Roach town with her daddy to horse trade and buy shine from his uncle and grandpa June.

She was maybe fifteen or sixteen back then while her daddy was trading him and his cousin's would slip off with her to their grandpa's pond, she would let them take turns fucking her, she'd suck their dick she told them not to cum in her mouth she'd bite their dick, guess what Joe got his dick bit. He didn't care she could bite it again she let him put his dick in her mouth again.

She wouldn't suck his dick no more he just got to fuck her pretty red fuzzy pussy. That's the good old days he remembered now he's back in prison serving his second ten-year sentence.

She was working for the sheriff's office as a c.o at the old prison camp where he was at. on weekends he worked laundry, the laundry building was in the back near the wreck yard. He was the only one that did laundry on the weekend.

She worked every other weekend that worked out great for him she'd grew up into a beautiful red head damn she had body nice pretty ass and nice big titties, now she had a pink pretty shaved pussy at that time and prettiest pink nipples he'd ever seen. Time changes everything and everybody.. That's fact's something we can't stop that's time and the way time changes everything.

Tamika ask if he fucked her in the laundry room? He said he did but not until he sucked her pussy. He'd rather suck a pussy than fuck it a lot of times. he likes the taste of pussy juice and pussy cum.

That's his favorite thing about a woman that's why guy's can't figure out how he's always with the prettiest woman, cause he's different than most of them he likes to suck a girl off fucking them with his big dick that's just for extra credit. That he can get at any time he wanted.

Tamika ask as she laid back on the sofa in the living room with her leg's open, would he suck her off like he did the red head? He said sure she laid back he went right for her shaved pussy just as he did the red head.

Him and Tamika had a good relationship he told her everything except the things he and a certain older lady name Dare experience together. Tamika wanted badly to know about this older lady name Dare. Dare was also a red head things they did Dare swore she take to her grave. Tamika wanted to know she wanted him to tell it so she could get off like she knew she would, In her mind she knew she just wanted to hear it from him he still would not tell, she'd keep on trying she thinks he will eventually tell her.

Just have to wait read and see if he does or not. If he does it's going to be worth waiting to hear about.

Chapter 16

Tamika and Joe met up at Day's inn one Friday after Tamika got off work. Joe had a room waiting on her to show up.

That's where you go to find what you looking for. Back side was called the ghetto side of Day's inn. Any thing goes on the back side at Day's inn.

This is where she could always fined him if he went missing in action. That use to happen often with him she would call she would text he'd not answer, he knew when she couldn't reach him she'd be bye there looking for him, that's how he played his cards to get what he wanted she would give in.

With the unlimited supply of crystal meth he could get his hands on for cheap now he was plugged in with Mexicans. There was always pretty girls around. That's how she use to find him laid up at the hotel selling meth and fucking young women.

She'd come looking for him in the passed she'd be pissed to begin with but like always he calmed her down with his charming ways. This happen often at Day's inn. But now he had changed it was all about her. Because anything he wanted to do she enjoyed with him.

She showed up after work she walked in he was setting on the king size bed rolling the bubble getting high as fuck, he took a hit then blew out a cloud of smoke that would over dose a elephant. That was his thing smoking crystal meth. Crystal meth was way better than Viagra he thought.

She ask him why he hasn't answer her calls? He said don't start just get naked and get on the bed. She liked when he told her what to do. She did what she was told she undresses then gets on the bed his dick is already hard from him jacking it with platinum dick oil. And smoking crystal meth.

He gets on top of her the head of his dick already knows where to go as she feels the head of his dick start to disappear inside her, her eye's rolled back at the way it felt so fat long inside her, he starts kissing her lips he grinds his body against hers.

He's in the move for some of what he knows black folk kinda loving. He kisses her lips while he grinds his body to hers his hips between her legs side to side working inside her thighs. This is old school baby making love. She mons soft he grinds slow getting every inch of his dick as deep as he can inside her.

Then he starts whispering into her ear a lot of ungodly things with her eyes close and him grinding her pussy, she fantasies about what he's talking about in her ear. He first talked about that red head that set on the wash machine in the laundry room where he was locked up , he tells her how pretty and pink her pussy was, Tamika mons as he's whispering all this in her ear.

She said softly don't stop tell me more, he told her how he sucked that pretty red pussy clit until she squirted in his mouth, Tamika said o yes tell me more did you fuck her Tamika ask with her eyes close.

He told her he laid her on the laundry bags that he had wash on the floor, then he put his big brown dick in her little white shaved pussy.

The red head raised up enough to look down and see what big brown dick was inside her white pussy then she lays back her eye's rolled back in her head.

Tamika said softly like this she raised up enough to look down and see what big brown dick was inside her white pussy, she lays back her eye's rolled back in her head. He said yea just like that!!!! Then Tamika eyes rolled to one side she said her it cums did you come in her? He said yes, Tamika said cum with me that's when she cum all over his dick he unloaded inside her his dick started going soft her pussy pushed his dick out his dick slides down her ass crack onto the bed sheet then it leak more until it was completely soft.

He lay there on her for a minute because she said please don't move just lay on me, so he did just for a minute then he got to his knee's between her legs he's got enough dick to start off again fucking her with his soft dick.

Not many guy's she said can do that he could he like the way it felt soft inside a wet cummy pussy, even if it wasn't his cum he fuck it anyway that's just how he was more different than any one else, she knew how different he was than any guy she knew.

While stroking his soft dick inside her cummy pussy he talk dirty again in her ear. This time he talked about her pussy being full cum that someone else come in her pussy before he put his soft dick inside her. She like what he was saying she ask him who was this guy that cum in her pussy before you put your soft dick inside her?

His dick was growing hard fast during this sex talk conversation. Joe's dick is a freak this is what it likes, most guy's either don't know or lie about what they think about that makes them get off.

Joe feel's he don't have to lie if a women is fucking Joe if she don't know she's about to find out, he's the one anything goes no matter what.

He ask Tamika who fucked his pretty little white pussy? She Whisper's I can't say if so you will be mad. He said to her was the dick bigger? She said in a whisper yes much bigger. Joe's dick was growing to its full peak with everything she was saying Joe is a freak, he wanted to cum he could feel it pump when she said that, not much more he could take he was going to cum.

He ask her again who was it? She said you promise not to get mad? He said yes I promise, She said you remember Q the black guy with the big fucking black dick that you double dick me with?

He said yea Q Diamonds brother, Tamika said yea him he's been the one fucking me. When she said that they both got off . Once her pussy pushed his dick out he rolled over beside her on the bed he lit a cigarette.

She looked over at him she said that was great let's do that more often. He would learn she wasn't joking she was really fucking Q the black guy he first double dick her with.

Chapter 17

Laying there she said to him it was when he ran off to Florida with Anna. She looked up Q on face book she ask if he had seen him? Q said no. She said that's when she ask Q if he wanted to fuck her? He said yea. He's been coming to her work fucking her every Thursday on the sofa in her office. Tamika said to Joe she wanted him and Q to double dick her pussy again just like before? He said OK.

Tamika ask him to tell her about this girl Q told her about Lauren Joe has been fucking all along.

Chapter 18

You want to hear about a Lauren he ask? Lauren he was foolish over. She didn't hide nothing she wanted to do. She was a wild girl some might say she was a sex Attic. She wanted different dicks everyday she was one he couldn't keep up with, the thing's she would do with him he'd never had a girl like her before. She was plum foolish over a black dick she was a beautiful white girl. She had no problem finding a black dick to fuck. She was foolish over Joe because he'd double dick her with the black guy's.

When he says guy's he means more than one. One night at Day's inn he got back from going to reup, he nocked on the door for her to let him in. A black guy open the door it was three other black guy's on the bed with Lauren.

When she wanted black dick she'd say to Joe you know what today is? He'd say what day is it? She'd say niga dick day, she meant what she said she was going to find one two three or four niga dicks that day to fuck her Joe would be there fucking her too. That's what she wanted.

That night he got back from going to reup when he walked in Lauren look like she was tied up with niga dick. when they were done him and the black guy that open the door Rayshon they was standing there naked with their hard dick ready to double dick her when the others were finish. This was the way Lauren was and what she liked about Joe he was a damn fool over that girl.

How many guy's are good with that? That's why Joe Roach is always with a pretty girl. Women like to have fun and experiment things like this not many get to.

Most the time if they do it's with another girl to make their man happy. Once again there it is guy's are all about them and what they want a girl to do.

Joe just goes with the flow Sky's the limit no matter what it is he's down with it. This and much more twisted things he started doing with Dare when he was a teenager. What's twisted to a lot of people is normal to him. After being introduce to these things at such a early age.

Dare said try it if he didn't like it they didn't have to do it again he's not stop from the first he tried it, If this is corrupted behavior Dare turned him on to it gets way deeper than this.

Dare's family was always like why in the hell is she so damn foolish over that young boy? She told them it was his dick size that wasn't the only reason, it was the things he'd do with her on the low that no one had a clue except the one's they did it with.

That's why she was so damn head over hills foolishly in love with him. If that got out back then in the eighty's both would been lynch by the neck that's how time has change over thirty year's. That's how all this in his life came about, when he was seventeen years old that's how young he was when he got introduce to doing these things.

What was forbidden then is normal nowadays to a lot of people. If it's not normal it's just the way it is, this was the story he told Tamika but with her he went into more detail of all the things him and Dare did.

Twisted by Joe Roach

When Thursday came he showed up at Tamika office like she ask him to. Q was there already Joe was wondering why Q hadn't been around, he figured Q had got plugged in with some other supplier, it never crossed his mind Q was fucking his girlfriend Tamika.

Tamika came out of her office she turn the sign on the door from open to closed she locked the door, she said OK guy's come on in my office. They followed her in to her office she shut and locked her office door.

She got undressed it was always a pretty site to see her naked she was a real and true beautiful blonde. To be forty years old she had a body like a twenty-year-old. Her titties were big and perfect size 40 DD.

She set on the sofa she lean forward with both them standing in front of her naked, they hadn't waisted no time getting undressed. She took both dicks in her hand she looked up at both them with her hassle eye's.

She put the black dick in her mouth first while she suck Q's black dick she jack Joe's big brown dick in the other hand with platinum dick oil. they both watch she wanted them both to get off first before double dicking her.

That way they wouldn't cum to quick with both dicks pumping and jacking against the others inside her tight pretty white pussy. First Q cum in her mouth then she finish sucking Joe off.

They took a break for about ten minutes then she help them both to get hard again. Her pussy was dripping wet just from knowing what was about to happen. Where she was setting on the leather sofa was a wet spot from her pussy dripping wet.

After she had them both hard. She had Q to lay on the sofa so she got on top after drenching his big dick with dick oil. She straddles Q while Joe watch from behind Q"s black dick disappeared inside her pretty white pussy. She lean forward arching her back while her pussy Joe could see swallowing his foot long black dick. At first it bent a little then straighten as it disappeared inside her until her ass was against his black balls every inch of his black dick was inside her white pussy. She rock back and forward on his dick to loosen her pussy before Joe attempt to put his dick in.

Chapter 19

Joe drenched his dick with dick oil stroked it good until it was as hard as it was going to get. It would have to be rock hard to force it's way in with her pussy already full of black dick.

Took a few attempts before her got the head in, She grunted then arches her back even more to make more room for his dick and for him to see his dick slide inside her pussy press tight against the black dick. Once it was inside she said to Q don't move let Joe do all the work while he's stroking his dick deep in her double dick filled pussy it will jack pumping against Q's black dick.

It only lasted five minutes she cum at the same time they both cum inside her, their cum shot out under pressure because of the tight fit. she could feel both pumping their cum inside her she instantly got off again. As their dick pump from hard to soft Q's push Joe's dick out before her pussy pushes Q's dick out.

Not many women have experience this because they don't have a man to experience it with. If anything women that get to experience thing's with their man it's most the time with another woman. Cause that's what the man wants. Women just trying to keep their man happy .

Joe has been the opposite for the beginning when he was introduced to doing these things, he was young and the woman that he started doing these things with took him in and took care of him so he did the thing's she wanted to do.

That was Dare soon after they met she felt he was the one that she could experience all the thing's she fantasies about in her mind during sex. She made a deal with him everything they did stayed between them she would buy him anything he wanted if he'd do all these thing's she want him to do.

He agreed because with her life was so sweet, Dare first open her safe in her bedroom to show him over $100,000 in cash she had put back. She said to him she would spend this money on him as long as he agree to everything she wanted him to do with her.

What he was agreeing to would turn him into the person he is today. What most people think is Twisted is everything he enjoys doing. If it's not twisted it's like it gets boring to him quickly.

Dare was always infatuated with big dicks if she heard about a guy that had a big dick she had to see it no matter the color or the cost that's just how she was.

With Joe having a big dick like he had at such a young age he was the one to do all these thing's with. Once this started things they got into was way more than most could imagine. Yea they got into so doing so many ungodly things together. Once this started it's was a addiction to do more and more ungodly things.

There was never no limits to what they got into often than you would think. If you want to know all the things they did just use your imagination believe me you going to need a Twisted imagination to get the full effect of the things they did behind closed doors with other guy's Dare pick to do these things with her and him.

Being Twisted is something he was introduced to forty years ago with her he liked everything they did he's continued to do these things his whole life. A lot of the women he meets like him because he's more different than anyone else they have ever met.

This has always helped him with being with a lot of women. No one else will ever tell the things or do the things he would do.

That's where his way of being first started and still he's that way forty years latter so you only can imagine.

These stories that he's telling are nothing to a lot of the things that did go on throughout his life. It's more to come more twisted than ever you will see bye the time you finish this book. So buckle up for the rest of the wild and crazy ride that he's about to take you on you just getting to the good parts of his twisted ways.

Back to Tamika.

After being double dick bye Joe and Q for the second time Tamika slowed her roll after finding out eight weeks latter she was pregnant.

She text Joe the day she found out after going to the doctor one morning before going to work.

Her daughter now five months along she was seeing a guy that thought he was the baby Daddy.

The whole time Tina and Joe knew who the baby Daddy was. At first Tina was trying to do the right thing being a good woman for this guy that thought he was the baby Daddy.

Now five months along while her mom's at work and her boyfriend also at work, she's walking around the house five months along in her panties and a short cut off shirt. Her ass so fine he wanted to fuck her in her ass.

He knew her pussy had to be dripping wet because all most pregnant women were, He kissed her on her lips that loosened her up he took her panties off, she laid down on her belly on the sofa he straddles her legs from behind just below her fine pretty ass he spreads her ass cheeks with his dick drenched with dick oil he rubs the head of his dick against her asshole.

At first she said no not my ass he said just relax he slowly help the head in with his hand cause at first his dick was trying to bend and slide up her ass crack, so he held his thumb behind the head until it slid inside her ass. Once the head was in he stop to let her asshole relax and get comfortable. Takes a minute once it's comfortable he takes it out then starts over, now it goes on in much easier once the head is in the asshole starts gripping and pulling his dick inside as he watch his dick disappeared as her ass helps the rest of his long dick inside her ass. Where does it go to take all that dick. It goes somewhere cause she takes it all the way to his balls.

He doesn't stroke it he just rocks back and forward until he cums while he's rocking it slow she has her arms beneath her pregnant belly play with her pussy clit, when he cums she feels his dick swell with each pump of cum pumping inside her ass she cums.

Chapter 20

When he finished pumping his cum inside her pretty ass he unstraddles her then gets to his feet. she gets up she said she needed that, she is one of those girl's that like dick in her ass as much or more than in the pussy. Rarely you find a girl like this just know you blessed when you do.

He checks his messages on his he see's he has one from Tamika and another from the preaches daughter. He checks the one from the preaches daughter first.

She wanting him to come pick her up she's at a friends house. He text her back to tell her it would be a couple hour's but he'd be there yes he'd been missing her also.

Anna text him back with the address to where she was at and said she'd be there waiting on him to get there, she said bye the way I think you might like my friend she wants to hang out with us also if that's OK with you?

He text back to say that's fine. Then he checks his message from Tamika. To find out Tamika is pregnant she tells him not top say anything to Tina she wants to be the one to break the news to her.

He calls Tamika to let her know he was going to Florida he'd be back as soon as he could. She didn't like the idea of him going his self she said for him to take her daughter with him.

Joe assured her he'd be fine he was going there and straight back she didn't like it but she said OK just hurry back, they needed to talk when he got back.

She said she wanted to do thing's different now she's pregnant. He said OK they'd talk when he got back. He showered the got out the shower on his way to the bedroom he rub Tina on her pretty firm ass.

Then he called her into the bedroom where he laid on the bed with his dick soaked with dick oil jacking his long fat hard brown dick. Tina takes her panties off she mounts him on the bed she takes her hand she guides his dick inside her hot wet pregnant pussy.

She rides she rocks back and forward on his dick until both are ready to cum he cums in her wet pregnant pussy she cums all over his big brown dick. She said to him I hope you know I'm in love with you Joe?

Her hormones kick in she starts to cry he kisses her lips holds her for a minute then tells her he in love with her also. He doesn't tell her he's going to Florida because he knows she will want to go with him.

plus he wasn't going to Florida to begin with. He was buying a couple day's to spend with the preaches daughter. He gets dressed he kisses Tina he tells her he had run out he'd be back.

He gets in black on black BMW convertible he put's the address in his phone the preaches daughter had sent him to were she was at.

When he gets there her and her friend comes out she's fine as fuck her friend is even more finer than her. They get in Anna ask what has he been up to?

Chapter 21

Before he could answer she said how his your relationship with the therapist going? He knew she'd been doing her home work to know about him and Tamika to know Tamika was a therapist.

He ask is this going to turning into a argument already if so he would take her and her friend back to her friends house and drop them out?

Anna said No she was good with him seeing the therapist her and her friend was just wanting to hang out with him get a room party with him get high have fun that's all they wanted?

He knew Anna she wasn't about to let it go that easy, with her beauty and her friend being more beautiful than her he was good with getting a room and partying with them. He had aplenty of crystal meth to have a hell of a time with these two girl's.

Her friend said hey bye the way my name is Teresa, Anna has told me so much about you and that trip to Florida you'll took for her birthday.

He ask Teresa how old was she? She said her and Anna was the same age eighteen. That he was glad to hear because of the ungodly thing's that was going through his mind that he'd like to do with her and Anna.

He was excited to her she was eighteen now he felt more comfortable with getting a room for the three of them to party get high and do the thing's he like doing with beautiful young lady's like her and Anna.

He ask her if she'd done crystal meth before she said she had, then Anna spoke up to say Teresa had done crystal meth with her and this guy she'd been fucking.

Joe knew where this was going so he went with it. Young girl's like Anna would say things like this just to get a reaction. Joe said to Anna who's this guy you been fucking? meanings she wanted him to know she'd been fucking another guy.

She said to him he knew this guy, she met him on face book after seeing him on Joe's face book page she hit him up. That puzzled him who could it be he had many friend's on face book.

Joe wanted to know who this guy was she been fucking? When he ask who? She smiled at him then said she's not telling. She knew what she was doing she said she'd tell him one thing about this guy. Joe said what's that? She said he had a massive size dick. Then she said to Teresa doesn't he Teresa?

Teresa said the biggest she's had, Joe pulls up at the hotel on the hill in Altavista. Anna said see if room 104 is available that one has a hot tub with a king size bed.

That was the room this guy she'd been fucking got the night he fuck her and Anna with one of his friend's. So you was with him and Teresa was with his friend fucking in the same bed at the same time Joe ask?

Teresa answers and said no the guy she was with fucked her while his friend was fucking Anna. So you'll switched out he said? Teresa said you could kinda say that except both of the guy's ended up double dicking both of them after getting them high on crystal meth.

Joe ask for room 104 it was available so he got that one, once they were inside the room he set on the sofa took out his bubble and a ounce of grade A crystal meth he had in his pocket, he loaded the bubble with damn near a gram off crystal meth. Then he put it to his mouth to take the first hit of crystal meth. He then blew out a cloud of smoke big enough for the three of them. When he blew out the cloud of smoke the meth was so good his dick cum while still soft in his jeans.

That's when you know you got grade A crystal meth. Not only did he get off everything went black ten seconds latter his vision came back. Teresa and Anna both said they wanted to get a hit that would do them like that.

But first they undressed completely they set on the sofa Joe held the bubble for both of them to get the hit like the one he just got. When he took the bubble from Anna's lips she laid back she removed her hands from over her pussy, she blew out enough smoke to overdose a elephant, her pussy squirt cum on to the coffee table in front of the sofa that's how good the meth he had was. Teresa was holding her breath just as she had took a hit watching how much smoke Anna blew out. She was wanting a hit like that to make her pussy squirt cum like that.

Joe wanted her to get a hit like that so she could squirt her cum in his mouth he wanted to taste her cum so bad he could taste it already.

He held the bubble for her the same way as he did for Anna when he took the bubble from her lips he reach it to Anna to hold as he went down between Teresa's leg's as she laid back on the sofa she squirt in his mouth so much he got choke trying to catch as much as he could swallow. Her pussy cum was so sweet it tasted like pineapple's.

These are the moments he wish would last for ever. Most guy's would never experience this life in a life time. This life style is life he lives for. Never had he tasted cum as sweet as hers. Her pussy was so pretty it should be against the law to have a pussy as pretty as hers.

Why is it God picked him to bless to live this wonder life he lives everyday? God has to love him way more than any one else he knows. Thanking god with every breath he's now watching Anna& Teresa on that king size bed in the 69 position sucking pussy and licking each other's beautiful asshole. What life could be better than this when you high as fuck on crystal meth?

The good old days of ripping running trafficking cocaine with a lot of beautiful woman along with all thing's that came along with it like the wild times in many different hotels up and down the interstate back then. Back then life couldn't get any better, then came the life of Crystal meth.

When meth hit it was a whole different high. Do away with the Viagra just get a bubble and smoke crystal meth. No dick pill can do the thing's crystal meth does to the sex drive for the men and a women nowadays.

Anna & Teresa he watch making out while he drenched his dick in platinum dick oil setting on the sofa in the hotel room watching them two.

Chapter 22

With his dick drench in platinum dick oil he stroked it slow from the head to his balls. Watching Anna & Teresa in the 69 position squirting cum on each other's beautiful face, it wasn't long before his dick started Cumming this was what he like the most watching to beautiful girl's getting each other off while he's satisfying his self watching the enjoy each other.

When he was finished his dick went soft he continued to watch Anna & Teresa enjoy each other. Wasn't long before he rolled the bubble again that always jump start his dick to start getting fat again. After taking a hit of crystal meth he again strokes his dick while it was soft drenched with his favorite platinum oil, this was a feeling he like to feel as he watch his dick grow fat long and half hard again. He knows from being told by many women he has a pretty dick, it's browner than any white guy's women say they had ever seen at it's peak from his balls to the swollen mushroom brown head it measured to be almost less than a inch of being a foot long.

Lots of guy's wonder what is it about him woman like? He's a handsome guy with a dick not many guy's will ever have. Once word got out about his very unusual size dick and the color it was for a white person. Girl's enjoyed getting fuck bye him.

He's always getting blame for any and everything because the reputation he's developed over the year's fucking so many women. Guy's and lawmen will lie if that's what it takes to put him away in prison so they can feel their pussy at home is safe because he's not around.

For him his dick size is a and has been a blessing but over the year's it's cost him more harm than good. Cause the little dick lawmen and their sheriff have targeted him pretty much his whole adult life because they don't want him near any of the women.

With a dick like his he gets all the pussy when he's around leaving the little dick lawmen and their sheriff to have to do with out while he rubs a great and wonderful life in their face because he can. That's something they not having especially from Joe Roach.

Back to the hotel room where he's watching Anna and Teresa make out with his dick half hard in his hand drenched in platinum dick oil.

He gets on the bed straddles Anna stops sucking Teresa's pussy he puts his dick in Anna's mouth then takes it out to put in Teresa's pretty little tight white pussy. once his dick is inside Teresa completely he starts slow stroking her tight little pussy with his long fat brown donkey size dick.

He keeps his dick and balls groomed at all times for the respect he has for the girls. Anna takes one of his balls into her mouth she sucks it softly as he strokes his dick inside Teresa's pussy. She pops his ball out then sucks his other ball into her mouth she sucks it softly the same as she suck the other one. Then she opens her mouth wide to fit both balls inside, once they both are in her mouth she closes her mouth around his ball sack she tugs at his sack with his balls closed up in her mouth he could feel her breathing through her nose on his asshole.

When the asshole is teased like this it gets the cum boiling it wants to cum inside Teresa's pretty little tight white pussy. He buries it deep with his balls in Anna's mouth his dick throbs to start pumping cum but first Anna has to stop tugging on his balls before he can get off.

Anna pop's out one ball at a time as soon as one came out he could feel his dick start to cum when she pop's out the other his dick shot off like bullet inside Teresa's pussy. His dick goes soft Teresa's pussy pushes his dick out it drops onto Anna's mouth she opens she sucks from his dick what cum is left then she pushes his soft dick out of her mouth his dick is soft his balls are drain both resting on her face, he then leans back he sets on his feet on the bed. Tamika has been calling he isn't answering her call's this means one thing he's up to no good. Tamika knows him like the back of her hand he's surely up to no good.

He knows Anna's not going to shut up while he calls Tamika, so he just turns his phone off. That's only going to piss Tamika off that much more, what other choice does he have? Cause opportunities like this don't come along everyday not in a life time he's not about to mess these up bye talking on the phone. That's only going to piss Anna off.

More often than you'd think when you keep a unlimited supply of grade A crystal meth. Joe will deal with the consequences latter but for now he ask Anna & Teresa if they were ready to roll the bubble again? They rolled the bubble then relax for a moment they were satisfied they just hit the bubble lay back enjoy the high. Now and then Anna & Teresa would turn towards the other one and kiss maybe explore each other's titties and smack each other on the ass.

He doesn't say Anna is a preacher's daughter to disrespect a preacher, he says it because she was a preacher's daughter in real life.

Thing's people hear about a preacher's daughter being the wildest girl's this is living proof of one of those girl's. Her Dad didn't like Joe for who her Daddy said he was. As you know it's all his fault once again.

It's been five months since she has seen him you can't blame Joe for her bad behavior, she said as soon as she was in the car she'd been fucking another guy. That was to piss Joe off she should have known by now that only turned him on more. Joe is probably the only guy these girls had met that turned them on to taking two dicks in their pussy at the same time. If you haven't tried it you need to cause you don't know what your missing until you do.

Guy's blame him for the things he does like this with the girl's if they wasn't doing it with him they'd be experimenting with someone else.
He will take full responsibility for the girl's he's double dick the reason other guys don't is because they don't have the dick to do it with. There for he is a peace of shit.

Chapter 23

In thirty six hours from time he left Tamika he pulls back in the drive way. Tamika is at work his phone is still turned off he lays it on the shelf in the garage before he goes into the house.

Tina's set on the sofa she also pissed off that he didn't take her with him to Florida with him. She ask him why he's not been answering his phone? He tells her his phone is somewhere there he'd layer it down before he left and for got it. He said its probably dead that's why they've not heard it ring.

She said with a pissy attitude yea right you took another bitch with you to Florida. She said her mom was pissed off, he said what ever then he went to the bedroom. He get then gets a shower he gets out the shower dried off walk out the bathroom into the bedroom.

Tina's setting on the bed on her phone with her mom she reaches him the phone. Tamika first call's him a lien bastard he said fuck you bitch then hung up the phone reach it back to Tina.

He starts looking through his clothes to get something to put on. Tina gets up from the bed she starts to walk out. For some reason the further along she gets the more beautiful she gets, always walking around in just panties and thin cut off T shirt.

He says to her where you think you going? She said back to the living room. He says to her no you're not get them panties off and that shirt so he could see that pretty ass pussy and big fucking titties she had like her mama's.

She did what he said because she didn't want to piss him off any more than he was already. She got naked she stood there a beautiful pregnant young girl.

He walks over to her she goes to speak he shakes his head she quickly shuts up she's seen him mad like this before, she better off not say a word when he's this pissed off she'd learn that from times before when he was mad.

He rubs her pretty firm white tight ass then he feel's both her titties with his hand big pretty pregnant titties. he put's his hand on her pussy it's soaked from the aggressive way he's smacked her across her ass.

He tells her like this he said you little bitch get on your mama's bed on your back knee's up leg's open wide I'm going to suck that pretty dripping wet pussy until you can cum no more.

She turn towards the foot of the bed she went to climb on to the bed when he open hand smacked her across her pretty ass hard, he said stop right there you little slut so she stop half on the bed half off her feet still on the floor.

At this point his dick is rock hard he push her down flat on her face on the bed. While he had his hand on the back of her head holding her head down on the bed.

He takes his foot he put's his foot between her feet he force her to spread her feet apart. still with his left hand holding her head down on the bed, he steps to the side to whip her ass with his had the way bad girls like to be whip bye Daddy.

She knew what was coming she'd called him Daddy many times while he whipped her ass bent over just like this. She said no

Daddy no please don't whip me about that times come hard smack right across her ass. Leaving a blistering red hand print on her ass he smacked her again the same way. She knew not to make a sound just grunt with every hard slap across her ass. She says Daddy please I'm going to pee. One more hard slap across her ass she pee uncontrollable he takes his hand he rubs her pretty little wet pussy, then he licks his hand it's pussy cum he tasted on his hand.

He then tells her to crawl onto the bed and stay laying on her face, she does what she's told, he gets on the bed he mounts her just below her blistered ass that's now cherry red.

He takes his dick in his right hand he rubs the head up and down her little wet pussy until it is soaked with pussy cum. Then he put's it in her little wet pussy. She said to him Daddy fuck me please.

With both hands on her pretty cherry red ass cheeks he spreads her ass cheeks so he can watch his dick disappear inside her pretty pregnant pussy as he rock back and forward watching his dick fuck her pretty little pussy. She called him Daddy until he cum deep inside her. Daddy's little girl!!!!!

When he was done she called her mom she tells her mom they found his phone he wasn't lien it had been then laying on the shelf in the garage the whole time.

Tamika tells her to put him on the phone he says hell know fuck that bitch tell her to go to hell the way she had talk to him. She tells her to put her phone on speaker so she can tell him she's sorry.

She tells him she sorry for calling him a lien bastard he said don't worry about it he's been called worse, she tells him that's why she loves him so much because he is so different than anyone else SNES been with. She tells him she still wants to discuss her being pregnant when she gets home.

The rest of the day he hangs out with baby girl sucking her big titties kissing on her belly she tells him he's so good to her. She said to him how strange it was for her having a baby bye her siblings Daddy.

She let him know she broke up with the guy she was seeing, when he ask why? She said his dick was to small. He said can't no one fuck you like Daddy. She said she knew that she loved her some big dick Daddy.

He tells her while she's laying in moms bed he's rubbing her young pretty ass he wanted to fuck her in her ass? She said to him she been wanting him to she thought he'd never ask.

Laying on her pregnant belly he gets the platinum dick oil he rubs the dick oil up and down her ass crack caressing her asshole with his middle finger until she arch her ass up taking his middle finger inside her ass.

Then he takes his finger out he drenched his dick in platinum dick oil before he mounts her just as he did before. He rubs her asshole with the head of his massive long dick, she tells him Daddy don't put it all in at first just give her half of it to begin with.

Chapter 24

He starts by putting his thumb in her asshole first to get it more comfortable before he put's the head of dick in her ass. She ask him Daddy is my asshole pretty?

She had pretty asshole, she ask was it pretty and pink cause she had just bleached it the night before? He said to her she had a beautiful asshole. Her asshole was so pretty he put the head of his dick in easy and slow once the head was in he let set there and relax.

Then he takes it out before he put's it back in he takes his tongue he licks then tongues her asshole, she said o Daddy that feels good never had my asshole tongue before.

He mounted her again straddling her just below her ass he put his thumb right behind the head of his dick ass he helps push the head of his dick in her ass with his thumb. Once the head was in he could feel her asshole gripping his dick pulling it inside.

Once it got halfway he stop then he rock soft and slow until he was ready to cum. She said to him Daddy cum in my ass. his dick pump his cum inside her asshole it pump it pump she said o my god daddy I can feel your dick Cummings.

Living there with Tamika and her daughter he felt was another blessing from God, two beautiful women both pregnant he's got it made no work all play. Everyone that knows him assumes he's fucking daughter anyway. Joe's been a hound dog his whole life, that's not going to change Tamika knows that.

While Tamika is at work him and her daughter are always together. Tina a drug free young girl enjoys the life of hanging out with him while he's transport's crystal meth throughout four counties. It turns her on just to be with him knowing they both are doing wrong, her knowing he's transporting drug's is one thing, getting pregnant bye him while he's with her mom that's wrong.

Joe and Tina shower together before Tamika gets home from work, he likes taking a shower with Tina it's nothing more beautiful than taking a shower with a pregnant woman. He likes rubbing her big pregnant titties with soap then watch the shower rinse them off. Tina has titties like her mom now they filling up with milk, her nipples stay hard because they want to be sucked.

Her ass is pretty and round like a bubble butt that's how a pregnant woman's ass gets when she pregnant, fucking her in the ass makes her ass grow into a bigger bubble.

Her pussy stays wet just as all pregnant women he's done fucked does. Her mom's not that far along yet but soon she will be, he can't wait to cores her big titties and fuck her in her bubbled ass. He knows he's one blessed guy to be able to live the life that he does. He's not in a hurry for time to pass he likes to enjoy his life one second at a time.

It's nothing like fucking a pregnant woman in the shower everything about a pregnant woman glows when it's a baby inside her. God continues to bless Joe everyday with beautiful women.

It's like God blessed him with all the right tools and the knowledge to bless so many women. Guy's and the lawmen aren't to happy at the life he lives.

It's like they are nothing but Hater's because they can't please the women the way he goes way beyond to please a woman. He can't help god chose him to be the one to be the way that he is.

Being this way makes it hard to live a honest life because of the Hater's and the lawmen are always out to take him out. Because they can never be like him.

When Tamika got home he was cleaning on his black on black BMW convertible. That was one sharp ride the young girls like riding in his car with the top down. At this time of year its been a while since he's rode around with the top down.

It was two weeks before Christmas his car was due a good cleaning especially the inside. Tina was in the house arguing on the phone with her x boyfriend she'd just broke up with last week.

Joe walked out of the house when her x kept asking her why she didn't want to see him anymore. He kept on until he pissed her off then she said, do you really want to know? He said yes please tell me?

She said to him remember you ask for this the reason I don't want to see you anymore is because your dick is to small. That's when Joe walked out to clean the inside of his car.

Joe felt bad for the little fella it is what it is, her boyfriend needs to except the truth then move on. Tamika ask him how was his trip to Florida? He said boring as hell since he for got his phone. He said bye the way thanks for all the fucked up messages she left on his phone.

She felt bad for what she had text him and said, she ask what would it take to make it up to him cause she felt bad for the messages she sent him. She said she was beyond pissed off she figure he was with a slut giving up her dick.

She said she was going inside to shower it's been a twisted day at work all day. He said to her he said was it Twisted as in Twisted like me? She said she didn't think anyone could be as Twisted as him then smiled kissed him then walked inside.

First thing first was a class of wine while she posted up at the bar, she couldn't help but hear her daughter argue with her x boyfriend about some dumb shit. When she'd had enough she ran her a tub to relax.

Joe walked in on her fingering her self in the tub, he just watch as she continued to fingering her pussy. She knew how to finger her self good, she could make her pussy squirt every time she fingered herself.

When she was about to blow she would switch from fingering her pussy to fingering her asshole. That's when she would squirt a gushing load of cum her pussy and asshole look so good the way she finger fuck them with her index and middle finger.

When she finish she laid her head back and said she needed that. Not many women play with their pussy in front of their man, she knew Joe liked it when she did. She knew how to relieve her stress.

Chapter 25

She relax for a moment then raised up setting in the tub he was turned on just bye watching her finger fuck her pussy and asshole.

Joe was one who like to watch a woman get her self off that turned him on, he had his dick out stroking it with platinum dick oil, that's one thing he kept in every room was platinum dick oil.

He steps over to the tub as he strokes his dick drenched in dick oil. When he was ready to get off she said to him cum on her titties!!!! After he cum while his dick was going down she open her mouth stuck out her tongue his dick rested on her tongue while it finished pumping it self until it was soft. She suck his soft dick in her mouth she tugged on it then popped it out just the way she does his balls when she sucks them one at a time.

A woman with soft lips knows how to sink a ship. She tells him she wants to talk to him when she gets out the tub he puts his dick up he shuts the bathroom door as he leaves out.

He sets on the Sofa with Tina he flirts around with her while her mom is getting out the tub touch her pregnant titties he likes the way she just let's him do what he wants.

She ask him if he was going to fuck her mom latter? he said he was sure that he would, she said to him leave the bedroom door open so she could come and watch. She like watching her mama get fuck bye him. Especially from behind when he has her mom's leg's on shoulders while he pounds his big dick inside her mama. See and hearing his ball's smack hard against her mom's asshole and ass cheeks that turned her on.

After her mom dried off she come out the bathroom naked she walks past them, Joe said damn girl you sexy as fuck he got up from the sofa an followed her to the bedroom. He left the bedroom door open.

Tamika sets on the side of the bed she starts telling him how she feels about not wanting to be double dick while she's pregnant, she told him he knew as well as she did when she got pregnant, it was when him and Q double dick her in her office and both cum in her at the same time.

His guess was as good as hers who the Daddy of the baby is going to be. She said she'd text Q to let him know Thursday's was off until she figured out what she was going to do about being pregnant.

He didn't text her back, Joe ask her what did she expect when she said she was pregnant?

Joe had no problem with what ever she decided to do she was his bread and butter, he lived with her she had her own therapy office. She made bank when it come down to the kinda money she made. She was a shrink that excerpted Medicare & Medicaid.

She owned her lake house she had a beautiful daughter that her mom pretty much raised until she finish school. Now she her daughter lived there with them, Joe done nocked her up her mom didn't know or did she know?

Joe told Tamika he was fine what ever she decided whether she was going to get a abortion or not. She said to him she was going to go through with her pregnancy that's what she was trying to tell him.

While she talk he stood in front of her playing with her big 40 DD titties. She said to him if he thought her titties was big now just wait until she got about eight months along.

If they were as big as they got when she was pregnant with Tina he'd see what a set of big titties was, cause they were massive size around her eighth month the last time.

He was a sucker for big titties he told her that would be worth waiting around for. She ask if he was going to be able to live in the house with two pregnant woman? Because her daughter didn't look like she was in a hurry to stay in a relationship long enough to get married or move out.

Joe didn't want Tina to move out he was enjoying her being there. He spent more time with her than he did with her mama. Now that Tamika mentioned no more double dicking while she was pregnant. Joe want to double dick a pregnant woman he'd not done that before.

This he would add to his to do list with Tina it's making his dick fat just thinking about double dicking Tina while she was pregnant.

Tamika come from a family of class she was a classy lady her self, classy women like doing trashy thing's as long as they can keep it on the low. Just like Joe & Q double dicking Tamika in her office.

What better place to be trashy than in her office behind closed door's. The same went for her fucking Q every Thursday in her office during the day.

Classy women like doing trashy thing's now and then, Tamika surely didn't want her daughter to know the thing's she was doing when she got pregnant.

Joe he didn't care what people said about what he's does, the only ones that had something to say was the Hater's and the lawmen. They were not happy at all knowing it was nothing they could say to make the ladies not have anything to do with him.

They have already said every ungodly thing they could think to say, everything they said he could agree with because he was the one that was ashamed of nothing he's done.

He was born and breed the way he is they just mad cause lots of women likes him the way that he is. Different is something he's always been. Different he will always be.

The ungodly thing's women can experience with him they know they could never experience with other guys. With him they have a great time doing every ungodly thing they could ever imagine.

With others they know better cause most men are some shit if ever they didn't get their way, they'd run tell everything whoever they are mad at has done with them before.

With Joe it's no limits to what they can do after it's done not a word is mention not even to them. The reason he's like this is because he knows as long as he don't tell no one most likely they going to do it again.

Ungodly things are way more fun than the everyday normal sex life, sex has a lot to with a relationship nowadays, if a woman tells a guy sizes don't matter. Just know that's a lie.

Chapter 26

Dare was who got him into doing all the things he gets into doing with women she turned him on to everything she ever fantasies about she had him to do it with her. It was nothing they didn't do together.

Not only did the older women love everything about him some had daughter's that liked him also. With Dare he got into a lot more with her than anyone else he was with. A lot of things they did only they and whoever it was with knows about.

She took him to the next level that's when he realized just how much fun being twisted really was. Dare had a fetish with big dicks his dick size and all the other thing's that she wanted to experiment doing with a guy she made him a deal he couldn't refuse.

He do what ever she wanted with her sexually he'd not have to work, she would spoil him with anything he wanted. She showed him at the time a brief case stacked with hundreds $100,000 in cash they would enjoy spending every dime of it as long as he did what she wanted?

He quickly agree to her terms, not knowing all the details what she wanted him to do. To enjoy $100,000 he didn't care let's get it on he was down for whatever.

Her family couldn't figure out why she was so foolish over him other than what she told them he had a eleven 11 1/2 inch dick at the seventeen. She was forty years old.

Twisted by Joe Roach

The thing's he'd do with her went way beyond that, Sometimes in real life sometimes with lots of sex toys. She turned bent in to twisted from the beginning he's been twisted ever since.

Like he said before lady's you know how in your mind thing's you would like to do with a guy that you've only thought about, because you have never had a guy you could ever trust to tell all the twisted thing's that got you off you thought about in your mind while being fucked.

With him you can do all those things that's the difference between him and any man you know. that's why he's considered Toxic to all women. Because of all they ever imagined doing you can enjoy doing with him. Without anyone knowing how twisted you both can be or have been. Sky's the limit you figure out why she was so foolish over him.

Just think how much money $100,000 was back in 1988. That was a offer he couldn't refuse. If being twisted is all it took twisted it was. One thing about the three years he spent doing any and everything she could come up with to do he had fun met a lot of people and learn many things. She kept her promise she take many things they did together to her grave as far as he knows she kept her word.

Dare is one woman he'll never forget all the ungodly thing's and everything else they had fun doing it. He has no regrets he learn one thing about life if you can't make yourself happy how would you expect to make someone else happy?

While hearing Tamika tell him the thing's she didn't want to do at least not while she was pregnant, he caresses her big titties as she sets on the bed in front of him naked with her feet cross in front of her. He agrees with everything she was saying. Even though he wasn't paying much attention to whatever it was she was saying.

While he caressed her titties with both hand's his mind was thinking about her daughter how he would like to double dick her while she's pregnant. Thinking about that was turning him on his dick was getting fat inside his Jean's.

He unbuttoned his Jean's he took his long fat brown dick out Tamika took it in her hand she tugged on it with both hands, she said to him shut the bedroom door. He ask why? She said Tina could walk in. He said so what she's seen us naked and fucking before.

He then said doesn't that turn you on for your daughter to see you getting fuck bye a big dick. She said quietly yes it does he pushes Tamika slowly backwards to lay on the bed his dick is rock hard.

He climbs between her leg's her puts his dick inside her once it's all in he whispers in her ear if it turns her on knowing her daughter was in the next room? She whispers in his ear yes it does. He grinds his dick slow to her wet lose pussy.

He whispers in her ear your pussy is wet and lose have you already been fuck today bye a bigger dick than mine? She whispers yes not once but twice I've been fuck today bye a bigger dick. He whispers in her ear does telling me that makes your pussy want to cum? She whispers yes it does, does it make your dick want to cum? He whispers in her ear yes it does.

He whispers in her ear tell your daughter to cum here. Tamika Whisper's in his ear OK , you want me to? He whispers do you want to?

She whispers yes. He whispers in her ear let me put your legs on my shoulders so she can see from behind your wet lose pussy take my long dick while my I pound your beautiful wet lose pussy, she can see my balls smack hard against your asshole?

She said OK put them on your shoulders hurry because I already feel like I'm going to cum just thinking about it.

He puts her legs on his shoulders he hooks his hands beneath her shoulders he can feel his dick go way more deeper inside her she mons.

Then she calls out for Tina and Tina answers yes mom what? Bring a towel hurry. Tina gets a to well from the bathroom she gets to the bedroom, her mom tells her to put the towel on the mattress the whole time Joe's pounding every inch of his massive long dick inside her mama, she puts the towel between them on the mattress.

Her mom begs her hurry and Tina steps back the towel is in place she see's how wet her mom's pussy is, her mom's pussy is making wet lose pussy sounds every time pounds it deep inside her.

Tina can see from behind his balls smack her mom's soak with pussy juice asshole his balls clap then he draws back for another hard clap to sound when he slams his dick deep inside her mom's wet lose freshly fuck lose pussy.

Chapter 27

Every time he drives his dick like a light pole into her moms wet lose pussy her mom's pussy spits an the noise's a pussy makes when it wet and lose her mom's pussy make those kind of noise's much louder than Tina's has ever made before.

She can tell her mom's pussy was a big wet pussy, Tamika screams o my God Joe pull it out I'm about to bust. He pulls his dick out as he sets back on to his feet with his ass her mom squirts so hard it looks like a water fall squirting out. Tina said o my mama I didn't know you was a squirter?

She's shaking her eye's rolled back her leg's relax as they slide past Joe on both sides of where he's setting with his ass on his feet. Tina watches her mom turn her head to left then to the right she jerks a couple more time's. Then she just lay there Joe's dick still hard Tamika opens her eye's she see's his long hard dick, her insides full of butter fly's. She says to her daughter it's a lot things about mama that you don't know.

She says to Joe fuck my daughter the way you fuck her when I'm not here. Joe looks at Tina and Tina looks at him she said to him told you mama's not dumb. Tina quickly pulls her T shirt off panties been gone, Tina with her beach ball pregnant belly and massive milk filled titties, she climbs onto the bed like a pussy cat from the foot of the bed to the head board.

She ask her mama mama how do you want him to fuck me from behind or on top like he fucked you? Tamika said the way he fucked me she wanted to watch her pregnant daughter take his long fat dick in her pretty little pussy that hasn't developed lips yet.

With Tina's legs on his shoulder's her mom takes his dick in Herr hand she rubs it up and down her daughter's little shaved pussy before finding her little pussy hole to guide the head in.

Tina's pussy is so wet when his head starts inside her pussy juice over flows soaking the head of his dick as it flows down puddling around her pretty pink bleach asshole, that he had just fucked only hours before her mom got home.

As his dick disappeared inside Tamika daughters' little pussy. Tamika places her thumb on Tina's pussy juice covered asshole.

Not knowing Tina's ass also likes to be fuck bye Joe's big dick, Tina's asshole sucks her mom's thumb and her pussy juice inside up to her mom knuckle.

Tamika takes her other hand as Joe pounds her daughter she clamps his ball sack above his balls in her hand, as he pumps his dick to her daughter, she clamps his balls and pulls is ball sack tight from the back.

With her thumb in her daughter's ass she explores her daughter's asshole with her thumb. Her daughter mons as she feels like she going to cum. Her moms thumb in her ass makes her want to cum faster and harder.

She pulls Joe's balls tight she holds them with a firm grip so his dick can't cum until she let's them got. Her daughter is swearing he's in to deep she can feel the head of his dick hitting her belly button inside.

She begs him not to go so deep but mama says fuck her daughter harder while he's pounding her daughter's pretty little tight white pussy. She cums with every long stroke cum gushed out from around his dick soaking her thumb in her daughter's asshole even more.

Joe's dick is pumping but nothing is coming out his balls drone tight in Tamika hand he starts to shake Tamika let's go of his ball he cum so hard it hurt the head of his dick when he shot a massive load that was built up before she released his balls. He'd never cum that hard before this was something new to him.

He rolls over collapse beside Tina he's done as they lay there Tina's pretty little pussy is winking at mama while it pushes out his and Tina's cum together. Mama goes down on Tina with her tongue and beautiful lips she suck and licks cum from Tina's pussy and asshole until she got every drop. Tina jerks to her mom's final lick from her asshole to the top of her little pussy slit.

Her mom set up in the bed she swallows she licks her lips she said to Tina your pussy taste so sweet. Tina lays there her thighs shaking uncountably. Her mom looks at the both of them she said before we leave this room all three of us going to come clean of all our secrets we been keeping from each other.

Joe doesn't have a clue what secrets she's talking about other than him fucking her daughter evidently she knew the whole time. Does she know Joe is Tina's baby Daddy? He's afraid to even get on that subject.

What all does she know and how does she know these things she about to tell him and her daughter?

There the three of them are on the bed naked Tina and Joe laying side bye side Tamika set on the bed between them. She ask who wants to go first? Neither of the Tina nor Joe offer to speak up.

Tamika said she would go first she get out in the open everything she knew about the both of them. Joe and Tina was listening they wanted to hear what she claim to know.

She started with Joe she said Joe you've done nothing but tell one lie after another, what you are is a compulsive liar. I don't believe nothing that comes out of your mouth this is the reason why.

She said the most resent thing is that trip you took to Florida yes the one you just got back from earlier today. You've not went to Flow you was in a hotel in Altavista for two day's getting high as fuck with Anna and her friend Teresa.

This fucked him up how could she know this unless she been talking to Anna that he couldn't believe was possible. She couldn't stand Anna because Anna was who he ran off with to Florida months back the first time he ran off.

She said to him you don't have to answer cause all you going to do is lie. Just know I know let's say a little bird told me. And know it was Anna I have nothing to say to than sinful little bitch so called preachers daughter, they the worst one's Tamika said.

Chapter 28

You been fucking my daughter ever since you and her took that 4 wheeler ride back in the mountain you know Joe the time you broke into the cabin then unlocked the door for her to come inside. Tina looked at Joe he looked at Tina who could have told this, then he quickly realized he had mentioned it to Q back when he first started fucking Tina while she was in school still.

Before Q and Tamika started fucking back when he ran off to Florida with Anna. But how did she know about Anna her friend and the hotel? Tamika said you trying to figure out how I know these thing's aren't you Joe?

She said let me finish with you both then I'll tell how I know. She said this is far from over especially you little girl she said to Tina.

She said to Tina Q didn't tell you all thing's he Joe Rayshon and some other black friends of his that's been fucking me? Tina said yes he told me what's been going on with you at Day's inn when you was supposed to be at work.

Joe's totally confused The only time Tina's been around Q was when Joe stop by Q's with her riding with him, that was before Q even knew her mom.

You want to tell Joe how many could be the Daddy to the baby you pregnant with better yet let me tell it Tamika said. Let's get all the secrets that we all been keeping from each other out in the open.

She said first of all let's talk about who's the Daddy is to the baby you pregnant with. Well your x boyfriend we know he's not the baby Daddy just a damn fool that fell for when you told him he was. Joe it could be yours. Joe the whole time just knew he was the Daddy to Tina's baby.

What he was about to hear is shocking to him, when it comes to being slick a woman can easily pull the wool over a guy's eye's.

Come to find out after spring break of Tina's last year in school, the reason she moved back home was because she was showing out at her grandma's. Sneaking Q and his buddy's in through the basement letting the have their way with her.

Not just Q not just Q & Rayshon She was letting Q Rayshon and Q's cousin gram all three have their way with her at the same time. Q told her mom Tina couldn't get enough black dick in her pretty white pussy.

Tina was a true and real coal burner had Joe snow balled the whole time. All this started with Tina the same time Tamika contacted Q looking for Joe the time he ran off to Florida.

Q's been telling Tamika everything. How did Tamika know about Anna & Teresa? Bye the way Joe Tamika said if you don't want all your white pussy being fucked bye your so called black buddy's stop bringing them around.

Anna and her friend Teresa bye the way being also fucking Q and his friend's just so that you know how I know everything.

Joe spoke up he said to Tamika thought you said you text Q to let him know Thursdays was off? She said she did text him yesterday which was Tuesday to tell him Thursdays were off.

Since you had so much pussy to take care of here fucking my daughter and everywhere else you go I just changed his day from Thursday to today Wednesday cause I was missing his big long massive black dick being inside me along with his two cousins Rayshon & Gram he brings them along for what you say extra credit.

That is why my pussy was way more wetter and loser today than it usually is I've been fucked and cum in bye three foot long nigga dicks. Just so you both know if you going to live here things are going to change around here dramatically.

Joe's never been one to get pissed off when he gets double crossed at his own game, he was the one to start this whole mess to begin with. To him it wasn't a mess cause everything that was going to hear Tamika talk about he needed his dick oil his dick was rock hard again.

He tells Tina to reach him the platinum dick like on the night stand bye the bed, she reaches him the dick oil he drenches his with the dick oil, Tamika looks at him she can't help from smile one thing about him she knew he didn't care he could get pussy anywhere. Knowing that it was hard to tell him no to whatever he wanted. Cause no woman wants to think they can't keep their man satisfied so he don't go somewhere else. Especially Joe because she would never find anyone like him again in a lifetime. He was more different than any guy she'd ever been with before she wanted to keep him around.

Tina ask her mom about these changes she's talking about starting today. Joe said first thing first he was going to fuck mama in her pretty white ass. While she suck her daughter's big pregnant milk filled titties.

Tamika said in what position he said doggy style position. Tamika got on her hands and knee's straddling her daughter so she could suck her daughter's big pregnant milk filled titties while Joe mounted her from behind just below her pretty ass he straddle her ass.

She said as he rub her asshole with dick oil then rub the head of his dick up and down her asshole and the crack of her ass. She told him it should be already lose cause Rayshon and Gram both had both took turns fucking her in the ass earlier with their big black dicks.

He knew Rayshon had long dick longer than his cause him and Rayshon had double dick Lauren at Day's inn before. So he knew if Rayshon been in her ass her ass would suck his dick in with no problem.

She arch her back like a broke back mule her ass up spread wide he didn't have to put his thumb behind the head to help it in her ass, her ass took the head of his dick so easy it was like taking candy from a baby. Once the head of his dick was inside her ass he could tell Rayshon had really fucked her in the ass. He like fucking her after another big dick done fucked her an cum in her ass, it was way loser and he could tell bye the wetness he felt as his dick disappeared inside Tamika ass.

He likes it when a woman's ass and pussy has been broke inn good he can pound away without having to hear anything other than cum in my ass Joe.

Chapter 29

With both hands above her hips around her waist he pounded away. knowing she been fucked earlier bye a bigger fucking dick in her ass that had his cum boiling to explode. Tamika sucking her daughter's big pregnant titties, with all this going through his mind, with in a minute he was buried up to his balls in her ass as his dick pump her ass with his cum he left in until her ass push it out as it went soft.

When Joe's with a woman you best believe it's a lot of twistedness going on in their relationship. This is the only kind of relationship he's interested in.

Woman like twisted as long as it doesn't get out, that's one thing they don't have to worry about with him, telling anything he will never tell cause he likes it to much. Why fuck a good thing up?

Tina pulled the wool over his eyes who turned out to be the baby Daddy was it Joe, Q, Rayshon, Gram,?

How did things change for him once he found out Tamika was taking dick from all his dope dealing so called home boys?

Did he stay or did he find a new girl to do all these twisted things with?

Twisted#2 coming soon read it to find out how many more are involved in all this twistedness that's been going on.

This is nothing Twisted is just getting started so buckle up for a lot more Twisted to come watch for the listing Joe plans to write Five different Twisted books. 1-5.

Remember what's Twisted to many of you is normal to him! Everyone gets into different thing's it's way more Twisted people out there than you think.

Just know he knows whether your girl's Twisted or not you may never know that you are with a double dick taking girl. especially if Joe's been hanging around. He's labeled the double dick bandit lady's young and older give a shout to him he lives in the Huddleston area Smith mountain lake Va.

If you never been double dick you don't know what your missing.

He writes as fiction to protect his self from the Hater's and little lawmen that pick at every word like vultures hoping to get a conviction.

Who knows one these women that likes being double dick could be one of their mama wife or sister who know but Joe and thee sweet little double dicking honey.

Just know dick size matter's when you got a beautiful woman means one of two things either you got good dick or you deep pockets.

Twisted #2 coming soon!!!!!!